"Let your prisoner go at once!"
Nancy demanded

NANCY DREW MYSTERY STORIES®

The Mystery of the Fire Dragon

BY CAROLYN KEENE

GROSSET & DUNLAP
Publishers • New York
A member of The Putnam & Grosset Group

ISBN-13: 978-0-448-09538-7

Contents

CHAPTER		PAGE
I	MYSTERY IN NEW YORK	1
II	THE DRAGON CLUE	9
III	CAMPUS SLEUTHING	16
IV	A DISAPPOINTING WAIT	26
V	A CONVINCING DISGUISE	35
VI	THE CHASE	43
VII	STRANGE THEFTS	51
VIII	ANGRY NEIGHBORS	59
IX	BESS IS MISSING	68
X	BOOKSHOP DETECTIVES	80
XI	A SUSPECT ESCAPES	89
XII	FLIGHT PLANS	97
XIII	AN OMINOUS DREAM	105
XIV	A HIDDEN MICROPHONE	116
XV	THE MAH-JONGG DEALER	125
XVI	A CHINESE PUZZLE	135
XVII	PURSUIT OF THE SEA FURIES	143
XVIII	A NEW ASSIGNMENT	154
XIX	SYMBOLIC FIREWORKS	163
XX	THE ESCAPE	172

CHAPTER I

Mystery in New York

"WHAT else does Ned say, Nancy?" Mr. Drew asked. He was listening intently to a letter his daughter was reading.

"Ned likes being a college exchange student in Hong Kong, and he has actually learned to speak some Cantonese, Dad!"

"Excellent. That, together with his study of Chinese culture, should make him very valuable in a number of fields," Mr. Drew commented.

Nancy nodded. "He'd like to go into the United States Intelligence Service." Suddenly her serious mood changed. "Dad, listen to this." She read, " 'Nancy, can't you find a mystery to solve in this far-off colony, so I might show you around?' "

Mr. Drew's eyes twinkled. "Mystery or no mystery, Nancy, you just might get to Hong Kong sooner than you think!"

"What!" the attractive, blue-eyed girl exclaimed. "You mean—?"

Before Nancy could finish the question, the telephone rang and she went to answer it.

"Aunt Eloise!" Nancy cried out. "How super to hear from you! Are you in New York?"

"Yes, right in my apartment. I want you to rush here. A most peculiar thing has happened. A real mystery for you to solve."

The young blond detective was intrigued and could hardly wait to get the details from her aunt.

Miss Eloise Drew, sister of Nancy's father, lived alone and taught school in the city. Her large old-fashioned apartment had been converted into two separate apartments. Each had its own entrance from the hallway.

"Two wonderful Chinese people moved in next door to me a few weeks ago," Aunt Eloise began. "We've become good friends. That's why I want to help them. There's a darling old man we call Grandpa Soong and his granddaughter Chi Che, an orphan. She's eighteen, and a student at Columbia University here.

"This afternoon, when I returned from a teachers' meeting, I found a strange note on the floor. It had been shoved under the locked door between my apartment and the Soongs'."

"And what did it say?" Nancy asked eagerly.

"It was short and unfinished," Aunt Eloise went on. "I'll read it:

Grandpa must think I am visiting student friends from Columbia. The police must not be notified I am away or Grandpa will be harmed. I am in grave danger because I have found out that—' "

"The note ends there?" Nancy asked.

"Yes, unfortunately. Well, you see why I need you here. I feel that Chi Che is depending on me to help her but I don't know where to begin. I thought you might bring Bess and her cousin George with you."

"I'd certainly like to, Aunt Eloise, but Dad has just been talking about a trip to Hong Kong. Hold the phone while I ask him about his plans," Nancy requested.

After hearing the story, the tall, distinguished-looking lawyer smiled and said, "We won't be leaving for Hong Kong for a week. In the meantime, go to New York if you wish."

Nancy hurried back to the telephone. "I'll come tomorrow, Aunt Eloise. What time will you be back from school?"

"Between four and four-thirty."

"I'll get in touch with Bess and George right away," Nancy promised. "And, in any case, I'll come."

"Good," her aunt said. "I'm really terribly worried about Chi Che. If much more time goes by, it may be too late to help her."

After saying good-by to her aunt, Nancy dialed

the number of the Marvin home. "Hi, Bess!" she said. "How about a quick trip with me to visit Aunt Eloise?"

"Sounds nice, Nancy. But why the big hurry? Don't tell me! I know—a mystery has popped up and the trail leads to New York City," guessed blond, slightly plump, Bess.

"You're partly right." Nancy laughed. "There is a mystery, but it started in Aunt Eloise's apartment." She briefed her friend on the details.

"Oh, dear, this really does sound dangerous!" Bess exclaimed. "Do you think we should—"

"Of course I think we should try to help Chi Che," Nancy declared. "We'll take the early afternoon plane tomorrow. I'll pick you up at one-fifteen."

"Okay. I'll be ready," Bess answered. "It'll be fun just to go to New York—shops, theater—"

"Bess," said Nancy firmly, "we have a job to do. Chi Che's in danger!"

"All right, Detective Drew. Deputy Marvin signing off. See you tomorrow."

Nancy chuckled as she called George Fayne. She was Bess's cousin but as unlike her in looks and interests as two people could be. Slender, with dark, short hair, tomboyish George was always ready for adventure.

Upon hearing Nancy's invitation, George was eager to fly to New York. "The mystery sounds intriguing," she said excitedly. "And, by the way,

Nancy, how about talking your dad into including me in the trip to Hong Kong?"

"I'll do my best." Nancy smiled as she hung up and returned to her father. "The girls can go with me," she said. "I'll make reservations, then please tell me about Hong Kong."

Ten minutes later father and daughter were again seated in front of the log fire which felt cozy on this crisp October evening. Presently they were joined by the Drews' housekeeper, Mrs. Hannah Gruen. She had lived with them for fifteen years since the death of Mrs. Drew, when Nancy was only three.

"Do sit down," Mr. Drew invited her. "I'd like to tell you about a case that may take Nancy and me to Hong Kong."

The pleasant-faced woman seated herself. "Oh, my! This sounds so exciting!" she commented.

"I have been retained," the attorney said, "to try to locate several people named as beneficiaries in a will which is being contested here. Their last known address was Hong Kong, but they don't answer letters sent to them by the executors.

"I've decided that the best way to find out what's happening is for me to go there. Naturally I'd like my detective daughter along to help me if necessary." He smiled. "And, naturally, a certain Ned Nickerson who is studying at Chung Chi College outside Hong Kong would like—"

Hannah Gruen laughed and Nancy blushed as

her father left the sentence unfinished. Then he continued, "Nancy, I'll come home from the office to lunch tomorrow and drive you and the girls to the airport. And now, if you two will excuse me, I'll say good night."

Promptly at one-fifteen the following afternoon Nancy and her father were at Bess Marvin's home. A few minutes after that they picked up George Fayne.

At the airport Nancy hugged her father, who wished the three sleuths luck. "We're ready for anything," George announced. "We even have our birth certificates with us in case we have to identify ourselves!"

"Good!" Nancy applauded. "I've learned while sleuthing to be prepared for anything. I always carry mine with me."

The girls waved as they boarded the airliner, then settled down for the flight to New York. When they reached the terminal in the city, Nancy led the others to the taxi exit, where they took a cab to Miss Drew's apartment house.

"Four-twenty," Nancy announced, as she pushed the vestibule bell to her aunt's apartment. The inner door clicked open. "Oh, I'm glad Aunt Eloise is home."

The tall, attractive woman met the three girls as they emerged from the third-floor stop of the self-service elevator. "You all look wonderful!" Aunt Eloise exclaimed.

*Something in front of Nancy exploded
with a loud bang!*

Nancy kissed her aunt a second time. "That's from Dad, and Hannah sends her best wishes, too."

As soon as they had entered the apartment, and the door was closed, the young sleuth said, "Aunt Eloise, don't keep us in suspense. Tell us everything about Chi Che and what happened."

Miss Drew produced the note the Chinese girl had written. At once Nancy noticed that in the lower right-hand corner of the stationery was a small hand-painted dragon in an Oriental shade of red. She pointed this out.

"It may be a clue," the girl detective remarked.

Aunt Eloise could add little to her story, except to say that the Soongs appeared to be very fine people and very fond of each other. They rarely had guests, because Grandpa Soong was at present spending most of his time writing a book.

"Let's call on Grandpa Soong," Nancy proposed, eager to start work solving the mystery.

Her aunt agreed. As Nancy opened the apartment door, she noticed a figure running toward the stairway. The person wore dark trousers and a loose coat.

Nancy stepped into the hall. At that instant something in front of her exploded with a loud bang!

CHAPTER II

The Dragon Clue

INSTINCTIVELY Nancy put both hands over her face and stepped backward into the doorway. Despite her quick move she was showered with a spray of paper and sandy particles.

"What happened?" Aunt Eloise asked excitedly. "Are you hurt?"

"I—I guess not," Nancy answered, as brownish-black smoke spread throughout the hallway.

Bess and George dashed from the apartment to look around for the cause of the explosion. Nancy joined them and a few seconds later held up a small tube. "I believe it was a giant firecracker someone set off."

"A firecracker!" Bess repeated, thinking that mysteries for Nancy Drew had started in many unusual ways but never before with a giant fire-cracker.

Ever since the time Mr. Drew had asked his

daughter to help him unravel *The Secret of the Old Clock* until recently, when Nancy had solved the mystery of *The Clue in the Old Stagecoach,* she had been in many precarious situations. The giant firecracker might have injured the young detective badly.

Nancy was staring at the Soongs' door. Was the explosion some kind of warning to the Soongs? Or, by chance, had someone learned that Nancy was interested in the mystery and used this means to scare her off the case?

By this time all the doors along the hallway of the apartment house were being opened and curious, frightened faces looking out. When the tenants found that no damage had been done and no one had been hurt, they closed their doors again.

The last apartment to be opened was the Soongs'. An elderly man, with a long beard and wearing a black Chinese suit, looked inquiringly at the girls.

Miss Drew stepped up and said, "Hello, Grandpa Soong. I want you to meet my niece, Nancy Drew, and her friends Bess Marvin and George Fayne."

Mr. Soong bowed low. "It gives me deep pleasure to meet the relative and friends of my very fine neighbor. I was on my way to answer the buzzer when I heard a loud explosion. Can you good people tell me what happened?"

"Mr. Soong, we think that a giant firecracker

was set off," Nancy replied. "Would you possibly know why?"

Grandpa Soong looked startled. "I know nothing about it. You think perhaps that because most firecrackers are made in Chinese territory I should know the reason?"

"Oh, no," Nancy replied quickly. Then she told about the figure she had seen running down the hall just before the explosion.

Grandpa Soong smiled. "Without a better description, I could not identify such a man or woman. But I am sure I would not know him, anyway."

The young sleuth went from door to door along the hallway, asking the various occupants if they had noticed the running figure. Each denied having seen anyone around.

When Nancy returned to the group, Aunt Eloise invited Mr. Soong into her apartment so that the girls might become better acquainted with him. Under the strong light of a reading lamp the elderly Chinese stared at George Fayne.

Suddenly he said, "Please forgive my rudeness, but you remind me very much of my Chi Che. Of course she is Chinese and you are American, but your hair, your flashing black eyes—even your dress reminds me so much of my granddaughter who is away visiting."

George was startled, not only because Grandpa Soong did not suspect that anything unusual had happened to Chi Che, but also that she herself looked so much like the missing girl. She glanced at her clothes and had to admit that her mandarin-collared overblouse did indeed look Oriental.

Aunt Eloise and the others seated themselves and almost at once Grandpa Soong began to talk about his writing. "My book has been many years in preparation," he said. "I spent much time in the interior of China gathering very valuable archaeological data. I hope my work will be of great benefit to mankind."

"I'm sure it will be," said Aunt Eloise. "Grandpa Soong, did Chi Che give up her after-school job at Stromberg's Bookshop?"

"Oh, no," the elderly man answered. "She loves her work and her studies. They mean much to her. I presume she has asked for a leave of absence from the shop while she is away visiting."

Nancy asked, "Did Chi Che leave you a note, Mr. Soong?"

"Yes." As he took one from the pocket of his jacket, he said, "I would cherish the idea if you girls would call me Grandpa Soong," and they nodded.

The note was written in Chinese characters and Grandpa Soong began to translate it. " 'Going on holiday with college friends. Home-coming indefinite.' "

Nancy had listened intently, but now her attention was drawn to a hand-painted dragon in the lower right-hand corner of the stationery. Curious, she mentioned it.

"This stationery is not the kind used by my Chi Che," Grandpa Soong explained. "It must have been given to her by the friend she's with."

He laid the note on the table, then went on, "The dragon is a very old and sacred symbol of China. The ancient name of the dragon was *Lung* and children believed in Lung just as Western children believe in Santa Claus.

"Legend tells us also that the dragon is the god of thunder. He appears in the sky as clouds which are said to be formed by his breath. Logically, then, the dragon is good because he produces rain and that, in turn, makes good rice crops, which are so necessary to the life of Chinese people."

The elderly man's audience was fascinated. Presently Nancy said, "So often when I have seen pictures of dragons they are accompanied by strings of pearls on the beasts or on the frames. Is there any significance to this?"

"Probably, but the story is lost in antiquity," Grandpa Soong replied. "The combining of pearls with dragons in decorative designs is an ancient custom, and while used principally in China, it was also used in the East Indies and Japan."

Grandpa Soong smiled. "I have heard that originally every self-respecting dragon had a pearl embedded under his chin! This gave him a special rank."

Nancy was thinking that all this information was extremely interesting, but the subject was not furthering her endeavors to glean any clue as to why Chi Che had left the note for Aunt Eloise implying she was in danger.

Finally Nancy said, "Grandpa Soong, have you a good photograph of Chi Che?"

The man's eyes twinkled. From a pocket of his coat he pulled a picture of a most attractive Chinese girl, dressed in a greenish-blue brocaded Chinese silk dress, with an inch-high tight collar.

"Chi Che *does* resemble you, George," Bess spoke up. "Of course her hair is arranged a little differently, but she certainly looks like you."

Grandpa Soong laid the picture on the table next to the note. Deep in thought, he paced up and down Aunt Eloise's living room, his hands behind his back and his gaze on the ceiling. Finally he turned to the group. "You will excuse me, I am sure," he said. "A thought just came to me which I must put in my manuscript."

Without another word he went to the door and out to the hall. "Oh, he forgot Chi Che's picture! And the note!" said Bess. She picked them up and started after him.

Nancy took hold of Bess's arm. "Wait! I'd like to keep the picture and note for a little while," she said. "An idea just came to me."

"A brain storm?" George asked, chuckling.

"I guess you might call it that," Nancy replied,

smiling. "I think the dragon is a definite clue. But before I tell you any more of my plan, I have another suggestion. I feel sure Mr. Soong as well as Chi Che may be in real danger. The person who lighted that giant firecracker rang Mr. Soong's buzzer. Perhaps he planned to have the baby bomb go off in the poor man's face. It might have blinded him! Anyway, I believe we should protect him as well as try to find Chi Che."

"I agree with you a hundred per cent," Aunt Eloise declared. "What do you suggest?"

Nancy said she thought they should obtain Mr. Soong's consent to keep the door between the two apartments unlocked. "We can run in every once in a while and see if he's all right. Also, being alone, he may not eat properly. How about inviting him to share meals with us?"

"I think that's a splendid idea," said Aunt Eloise. "But before I ask him, what is this other scheme you have up your sleeve, Nancy?"

The young sleuth smiled. "It's a very daring plan, I warn you."

CHAPTER III

Campus Sleuthing

"GEORGE FAYNE," Nancy said, "you are about to become Chi Che Soong!"

"What!" George cried out.

Nancy smiled. "I'm sure that with a little change in your hair style, you could pass for Chi Che. We'll shape your eyebrows and make them heavier. We'll place a bit of rouge high on your cheekbones and change that boyish hairdo of yours into a pixy cut."

Nancy picked up the picture of Chi Che. "Look at this photograph and tell me what you think."

After the others had studied it a moment, Bess gave Nancy a hug. "You're a genius. It wouldn't be hard to do at all, and if George puts on the dress Chi Che's wearing in the picture, I'll bet people will think she's Chi Che, at least from a distance. Nancy, what do you have in mind for George to do?"

Nancy said that first they must get Grandpa Soong's consent to keep the door between the two apartments unlocked. After George was made up, she was to leave by way of the Soongs' entrance. "Bess, you and I will follow at a distance and see if anyone is trailing her."

"You mean I'm just to walk up one street and down another and wait to be hit on the head?" George asked with a grin.

"Oh, do be sensible," Nancy begged. "I haven't decided yet where I'd like you to go. But please don't leave this apartment until you go out dressed as Chi Che Soong."

"I won't mind," said George. "There are some good books here to read. But you know me—I like action. So don't make it too long."

Bess now spoke up. "I was under the impression, Nancy, that you thought Chi Che was a prisoner. But if George is going to parade around the streets," she added, "this puts a different light on the mystery. You don't think Chi Che is being held after all, do you, Nancy?"

Nancy said she had not reached a conclusion as yet. "Chi Che may be a prisoner, or she may only be in hiding. But if the person from whom she's hiding thinks he sees her on the street, we may be able to find out something worth while."

Aunt Eloise and the cousins approved Nancy's idea and George said she would be willing to undertake the experiment.

"Then the next thing," said Aunt Eloise, "is for me to go next door and make the arrangements with Grandpa Soong." She left and the girls continued to talk about the mystery until her return.

"I had no trouble at all," Miss Drew reported. "Grandpa Soong was delighted to accept our invitation, and incidentally we are to call him when supper is ready. The door is unbolted now on his side. Come, I want to show you something exquisite."

Aunt Eloise went to the connecting door and unlocked it from her apartment. Directly behind the door hung a large silk scroll which reached to the floor.

"This is a perfect screen," Miss Drew remarked. "Anyone coming into the Soong apartment wouldn't know there is a door behind it."

Nancy and her friends squeezed past the scroll and stepped into the Soong living room. The elderly man was not around and Aunt Eloise whispered that he was writing in his bedroom.

"What a gorgeous hand-painted scroll!" Bess remarked, gazing at the lovely ancient Chinese garden scene with men and ladies strolling about.

Before leaving the apartment, Nancy and the other girls took a quick glance around. The room was tastefully furnished with a Chinese teakwood table, chest, and chairs. There were hand-painted parchment shades on the lamps, and the floor was almost entirely covered by a heavy Oriental rug richly colored in blue and tawny yellow and bordered with a floral design.

"There are two bedrooms and a kitchen," Aunt Eloise explained. "Grandpa Soong does all his writing in his bedroom."

Quietly the visitors went back to Miss Drew's apartment and the girls unpacked their clothes. Presently preparations for supper were started, and when everything was ready, Miss Drew went to call Grandpa Soong.

As she brought him in, the teacher teasingly remarked that it was hard to get him away from his writing. "Perhaps we shouldn't ask," she said to him, "but if we promise not to tell, will you give us an idea of what you were adding to your manuscript this afternoon?"

The elderly Chinese smiled, put his fingers together, and looked into space. "The manuscript is finished but I want to write a foreword. I am sure there is no harm in revealing the material I inserted. It is known to many people. In my archaeological work I dug up an ancient frieze. Until my book is printed no one will know its exact origin.

"On the frieze," he continued, "is pictured one of the early heroes of Chinese history—Fu Hsi. He lived over 4,800 years ago."

"Whew!" George cried out. "He's a prehistoric man, no less! What did he look like?"

Once more Grandpa Soong's eyes twinkled. "Fu Hsi had the head of a man and the body of a dragon!"

"Ugh!" Bess remarked. "I'm glad there aren't any such people around today. What did this man do?"

"Legend tells us that he was the king. He had six counselors, all of them dragons. In fact, there was a line of kings, called the Man Kings, who had faces of men and bodies of dragons. This probably explains why China has often been called Dragon Land."

"Where is this frieze now?" Nancy queried.

"In a museum in China." Grandpa Soong suddenly looked pensive. "I hope to be able to go back home sometime and see it."

As soon as the group had finished eating supper, Grandpa Soong expressed his thanks for their hospitality, then said he would like to return to his own apartment and do more writing.

By ten-thirty Miss Drew and her guests were sound asleep. All were up early the next morning. After Miss Drew had left for school, Bess said to Nancy, "What's on our girl detective's calendar?"

"I thought you and I might go to Stromberg's Bookshop and see if we can pick up a clue about Chi Che. If we fail, then George can take over."

The two girls set out, and after walking a few blocks, came to Stromberg's Bookshop. There was one woman customer inside, but no salesclerk.

Seeing the girls, the woman, who was portly and unbecomingly dressed in a ruffled blouse and bouffant skirt and carrying her coat on her arm, came up to them immediately.

"This is most annoying!" she complained. "I don't know where Mr. Stromberg can be and I'm in a great hurry. I come here often and it's always the same story. Nobody to wait on me!"

Nancy and Bess merely smiled, wondering why the woman bothered to come back if she were displeased with the service.

As if reading their thoughts, she said, "But Mr. Stromberg has such a fine collection of foreign books that I hate to go elsewhere." She smiled in a tolerant sort of way, however, and said, "But Mrs. Horace Truesdale is not one to lose her temper. No doubt Mr. Stromberg has a good reason for not being here."

"Doesn't Mr. Stromberg have a salesclerk?" Bess asked Mrs. Truesdale.

"I believe so, but she's a college student and doesn't work here full time."

The girls began to look around at the books on the shelves, trying to conceal their own impatience for the owner's return. Mrs. Truesdale kept up a constant chatter.

"Have you ever been to the Orient?" she asked the girls.

When they shook their heads, the woman went on, "I'm planning to go myself with one of the tourist groups. That's why I'm here—looking for books on the Orient."

Idly she picked several volumes from a shelf and started to leaf through them. "Oh, dear, where *is* Mr. Stromberg? I've been here ten minutes!" When the girls made no comment, Mrs. Truesdale said, "I suppose I'm an idiot to go abroad. Air travel doesn't agree with me. Besides, I hate being away from my family for such a long time."

Nancy and Bess smiled in spite of themselves. When Mrs. Truesdale moved away, Bess whispered, "I'll bet that woman's a pest. I should think her family would be glad to see her go away for a while."

Finally Mr. Stromberg came in from the street.

He was about fifty years old, of medium height and build, and had piercing blue eyes, a high forehead, and a prominent nose.

He nodded to Mrs. Truesdale, saying, "I have some books for you. Would you mind waiting a few minutes?"

Turning to the girls, he asked, "Can I do something for you young ladies?"

"Will Chi Che be here soon?" Nancy asked.

"I presume you mean Chi Che Soong. No," Mr. Stromberg replied. "Chi Che asked for time off— wasn't certain of her return either, so I can't tell you when she'll be in."

"Well, thank you very much," said Nancy. "I'll drop by again and see if she's here."

Mr. Stromberg gave a great sigh. "I wish Miss Soong would get back. We deal in foreign-language books and she was a great help to me. You know, Chi Che Soong speaks seven languages!"

"How amazing!" Bess remarked.

"Isn't there something I can do for you?" the shop owner asked.

"Well, not in the line of books," Bess answered. "We—ah—wanted to invite Chi Che to a party."

Mr. Stromberg, not interested in this subject, walked over to Mrs. Truesdale, and the two girls left the shop.

"We didn't learn anything there," Bess said.

Nancy frowned and admitted that she was frankly puzzled. Chi Che's note to Aunt Eloise had indicated that it was written on the spur of the moment and under great stress. Somebody she feared must have been nearby because she was unable to finish the last part of the note. Yet Mr. Stromberg said Chi Che told him she wanted time off and her return was uncertain. Nancy revealed her thoughts to Bess.

"The two things just don't dovetail," she said finally.

"It's too deep for me," Bess admitted, shaking her head. "Well, where do we go from here?"

Nancy suggested that they make a trip to Columbia University and try to find out something about Chi Che. When they arrived on campus, the girls went to the office of one of the deans. A young woman assistant proved to be most helpful. She suggested that the girls go to the building where foreign students often gathered.

"They may be able to tell you something about Miss Soong," the young woman said.

Nancy and Bess hurried to the designated building. It was almost lunchtime and the girls noticed everyone heading for the cafeteria in the building. Nancy and Bess stood near the door. Several Chinese young people came in. The American girls smiled at them and asked if they knew where Chi Che was. None did, and one girl added:

"Chi Che has been cutting classes lately. She never did that before. I can't understand it."

Nancy said that she had heard Chi Che was visiting college friends out of town. The Chinese student looked surprised. "None of her friends here is away. If she's visiting, the person must be someone from another college."

"Would you like to come and have lunch with our group?" the Chinese girl invited.

"Why, thank you very much," said Nancy. "We'd love it. I'm Nancy Drew and this is my friend Bess Marvin."

"My name is Amy Ching," the other girl said.

The three went into the cafeteria and Amy Ching introduced Nancy and Bess to several other foreign students, but none could give any information about Chi Che Soong.

Nancy and Bess returned to the apartment early in the afternoon and brought George up to date on their findings. Nancy remarked, "Frankly I'm worried, even more than I was before. Apparently Chi Che Soong had no idea while at school on the day she disappeared that she was going to be away."

At supper that evening Nancy and the other girls, as well as Aunt Eloise, forced themselves to be gay in the presence of Grandpa Soong. The door between the two apartments was left open

Later that night Nancy was in a deep sleep when she was suddenly awakened by a scream. As she sat up in bed she realized that the scream had come from the Soong apartment. The young detective jumped out of bed.

By this time Aunt Eloise, Bess, and George were awake also. They could hear moaning from the adjoining apartment.

They grabbed their robes, rushed into Grandpa Soong's living room, and turned on the light. No one was there.

Aunt Eloise led the way to the elderly man's bedroom. A desk lamp was on. In its rays they could see Grandpa Soong lying on the floor. He was barely conscious. As the group knelt beside him, he whispered:

"Stole—my—manuscript!"

CHAPTER IV

A Disappointing Wait

"WE MUST call a doctor at once," Aunt Eloise said. She asked Grandpa Soong who his physician was, but the elderly man was too weak to answer. Miss Drew turned to George and requested, "Please telephone my physician, Dr. Gordon."

Meanwhile Aunt Eloise, Bess, and Nancy gently lifted Grandpa Soong onto his bed. Then Nancy ran back through her aunt's apartment and out into the hall to see if the attacker were in sight. The young sleuth knew it was a vain hope, and as she had expected, no one was there.

Nancy realized that by the time she waited for the self-service elevator to come up from the first floor and take her down again, the thief would have made his escape.

Quickly Nancy ran down the stairs. She stopped at each floor and looked around for any sign of the thief. Finally, reaching the lobby without having seen anyone, she dashed to the front door and gazed up and down the street. No one carrying papers under his arm or a bundle or suitcase was in sight.

Nancy hurried back to Aunt Eloise's apartment, and using the kitchen phone, immediately called police headquarters. She was switched to Captain Gray, who was on duty at the nearby precinct. The officer said he would send two of his men at once to investigate.

Then Nancy returned to Mr. Soong's apartment to do a little investigating of her own. She found that everything had been stripped from the archaeologist's worktable except the lamp. A bottle of Chinese ink and brushes lay on the floor and near it an exquisite hand-painted metal vase.

Every drawer in the room was open and the contents were strewn about. Bookshelves were in disarray. Apparently the thief had made a quick but thorough search of Grandpa Soong's workshop for all papers, notes, and photographs pertaining to the manuscript.

The buzzer interrupted Nancy's investigation and she went to open the door.

"I'm Dr. Gordon," said the smiling young man.

Nancy led him to Mr. Soong's bedroom. Aunt Eloise and the girls withdrew while the doctor made an examination of the victim. As they waited for his report, the buzzer sounded again.

Two police officers had arrived. They introduced themselves as Brady and Reed. Upon hearing that the doctor was in the bedroom, the two men said they would start in the living room to search for a clue to the intruder.

Presently Brady said, "He didn't force an entry, so he must have had a key."

Finding nothing to help identify the thief, Officer Reed added, "Apparently the thief went immediately to the bedroom. From what you tell me, Miss Drew, Mr. Soong was working at his desk when he was attacked."

Just then Dr. Gordon appeared. He shook his head. "Mr. Soong's condition is the result of fear as well as a hard blow. He will have to be removed to the hospital at once."

"I'll call an ambulance," Officer Brady offered, and went to the phone.

Nancy asked the doctor if it would be possible for her to talk with Grandpa Soong before he was taken away. "Yes," Dr. Gordon replied. "But make it brief."

Both officers followed her inside and introduced themselves. The elderly man gave the girl a warm smile. "I am very grateful to you, my friend," he said in a whisper. "I—I do not know why my manuscript was stolen."

Officer Reed asked him for a description of his assailant.

"The man was masked," Mr. Soong said, "and wore a hat pulled low, so I could tell nothing about his face or hair. He was rather small, but very strong."

At once Nancy wondered if he might be the same person she had seen running away after the firecracker explosion. That person was small, too. She told this to the officers.

At that moment the door buzzer sounded. Two ambulance attendants carrying a stretcher entered the apartment. As they carried Mr. Soong from the room, his friends gave him their best wishes for a quick recovery.

As soon as the attendants and their patient had left, the two police officers went toward Grandpa Soong's bedroom. One of them carried a little kit which Nancy knew was a fingerprinting outfit.

"Do you mind if I watch you work?" she asked.

"No, come along," Officer Reed replied.

As she started to follow, Nancy was detained by Bess. "Don't you think we should tell the officers about Chi Che and our suspicions that she's in danger?"

George tossed her head. "Certainly not. Chi Che asked Aunt Eloise not to."

"Just the same—"

Miss Drew spoke up. "Bess has a point, but so has George. Let's take a vote."

Nancy and Aunt Eloise sided with George. Resignedly, Bess said, "Okay. But if Chi Che is still missing by tomorrow I'll probably ask the same question again."

Aunt Eloise smiled. "A lot can happen in twenty-four hours," she said. "You've already found that out since you came to New York."

Nancy went into Grandpa Soong's bedroom to watch the police officers. They had already opened their kit. One man was holding a camel's-hair brush and a bottle of gray powder.

"This must be one of the thief's hand marks," said Officer Brady, who was shining a flashlight on the desktop and looking through a magnifying glass. "The finger spreads indicate a larger hand than that of Mr. Soong's. And shorter fingers."

Officer Brady dusted the prints with the powder. Then, as his co-worker held the flashlight, he picked up a camera and photographed the prints.

Officer Reed turned to Nancy. "We'll get these prints two ways," he said. "Now we'll use lifting tape."

He took what looked like a large rubber patch with a thin outer coating from the kit. First he peeled off the coating, and Nancy noticed that the rubber under it was very sticky. He placed this over the fingerprint, then gently took it off.

"Very good," he said. "Come look, Miss Drew."

Nancy took a few steps forward and studied the perfect reprint on the tape. She smiled up at the officers. "It's fascinating," she said. "And now I'm going to ask you a favor. If you should find that these fingerprints are on record, will you let me know to whom they belong?"

"I guess we can do that," Officer Reed replied.

After the two men had left, Nancy and the girls returned to Miss Drew's apartment. "I'm going to bolt this door," Aunt Eloise announced. "I don't want any thieves coming in here!"

Nancy gazed into space for several seconds, then said, "Aunt Eloise, I don't blame you for feeling the way you do. But I think there's a good chance the thief or some accomplice of his may come back to the Soong apartment to try stealing something else. What I'd like to do is spend the rest of the night there and find out."

Miss Drew shook her head. "It's too dangerous," she argued. "I'd never forgive myself if anything should happen to you."

"George can stay with me," Nancy said, by way of persuasion. "I'll place a chair under the door handle so no one can possibly get in. If I hear anyone trying the door, I'll call the police."

George spoke up. "Why call the police? Why don't you and I just go out and capture the thief?"

Before Miss Drew could comment, Bess remarked, "It's just possible Chi Che herself will return and won't be able to get in."

"That's true," Aunt Eloise conceded. "Chi Che may have been held and her key to the apartment taken just so the thief could accomplish the job of taking the manuscript."

Bess's eyes sparkled. "And Chi Che will be released! Won't that be wonderful!"

"I wish I shared your optimism," said Aunt Eloise. "Just in case she should come home and try to get in, I'll permit Nancy and George to finish the night in the Soong apartment."

Bess went on, "Do you think the part of Chi Che's note 'Because I have found out that—' meant the plan to steal the manuscript?"

Nancy shook her head. "Unless Chi Che returns home tomorrow morning, my answer would be 'no.'"

Nancy and George slept fitfully the balance of the night. By seven o'clock they were wide awake. They were just about to go back to Aunt Eloise's apartment when the Soongs' door buzzer sounded. George jumped perceptibly. Without making a sound she formed her lips into the words, "Shall we answer it?"

Nancy shook her head. Beckoning to George to follow her, she led the way to the adjoining apartment, opened the hall door, and peered out cautiously.

Mr. Stromberg was standing at the Soong door!

Quickly and quietly Nancy Drew closed the door to her aunt's apartment. In hushed tones she told George about the caller. "Just as well if Mr. Stromberg doesn't find out where we're staying," she whispered.

Mr. Stromberg rang the buzzer again. Then, apparently deciding that no one was coming to answer it, he walked to the elevator.

"I suppose he came here to see why Chi Che hasn't returned to work," George remarked. "He sure gets around early in the morning."

Nancy frowned. "I wonder how Mr. Stromberg got into the apartment house. He didn't ring the downstairs bell to the Soong apartment."

George shrugged. "Oh, well, someone was probably just going out the lobby door at the time he arrived, and that's how he got in."

Aunt Eloise and Bess were already up, and Nancy and George became conscious of the aroma of broiling bacon. They went into the kitchen and reported Mr. Stromberg's visit.

"You were wise not to let him know where you are, Nancy," her aunt praised her.

About an hour later the telephone rang. "Will you take it, Nancy?" Aunt Eloise requested. "I'm sorry I forgot to tell you. I must go out to an all-day teachers' meeting."

Miss Drew paused by the door long enough to learn that it was a call from police headquarters. Captain Gray was reporting that the fingerprints of the burglar had been checked with FBI records. "Whoever the thief was," he said, "he has never been arrested."

The captain went on to say that his men had checked every tenant in the apartment house with the superintendent and also the renting agent in charge of the building. "We're sure the suspect doesn't live there," he stated.

"Thank you for letting me know," said Nancy. "And I am still very much interested in this case. If you have any further news, I'd appreciate hearing from you."

The officer chuckled. "I understand you are an amateur sleuth, Miss Drew," he said. "I heard this from Dr. Gordon when he called up to give a report on Mr. Soong. It seems your aunt had been telling him about you."

Nancy laughed. "I see I can't keep that a secret. Well, now that you know, I hope you won't mind if I try to solve the mystery, too."

"The department would be delighted to have your help," Captain Gray replied.

After clearing away the breakfast dishes, the three girls tidied up not only Aunt Eloise's apartment but also Grandpa Soong's. Time dragged as they waited hopefully for Chi Che Soong to return home. Near noon Nancy finally said:

"I'm sure Chi Che is still either being held prisoner or is in hiding. Whichever is true, we must find her! Let's have a bite of lunch and then start our sleuthing."

She turned to George. "Are you ready to play the part of Chi Che?"

CHAPTER V

A Convincing Disguise

"OF COURSE I'll play the part," said George Fayne. "But I must admit that I'm getting butterflies in my stomach."

The three girls decided to look through Chi Che Soong's clothes for the dress Chi Che was wearing in the photograph Grandpa Soong had shown them. As much as they disliked the thought of invading the Chinese girl's wardrobe, Nancy and her friends felt it was quite necessary if they were to solve the mystery.

Bess opened the door of a closet in Chi Che's bedroom. "Here's the dress."

As she removed the dress from its hanger she remarked how pretty it was. "And ummm, what a sweet sachet it's scented with—like incense."

"And now to find Chi Che's eyebrow pencil and rouge and lipstick, if she has any here."

George opened the drawer to Chi Che's dressing table. "We're in luck again," she said. "And look, here's a key. It might be a duplicate to the hall door. I'd better carry it, so I can let myself back in."

Nancy tried the key in the lock. "This is it all right. Well, let's go back to our own apartment now and fix you up, George."

It was easy to apply the make-up and have George slip into the dress, but changing her hairdo proved to be a difficult task. The ends just would not turn forward and stay in position.

"What do you put on your hair, anyway?" Bess chided her cousin. "Varnish?"

"No, cement," George replied impishly. Then she said the best thing to do would be to rinse her hair with water and set it while damp.

"But that will ruin your make-up and this dress," Bess objected.

"Not necessarily," said Nancy. "Come with me, George."

She led the way to the bathroom, put a towel around George's shoulders, and told her to lean over the basin. Quickly and carefully Nancy rinsed her friend's hair and partially dried it before George raised her head. Now Nancy found it easy to arrange a hairdo very similar to Chi Che's.

When she finished, Bess exclaimed in wonder, "I can't believe it! You really do look like the girl in this picture, George." Suddenly she made a low bow. "Delighted to meet you, Chi Che Soong!"

The girls giggled for a few moments, then became serious and discussed the route George was to follow. She would leave the Soong apartment, take the elevator down, dawdle in the lobby until Nancy and Bess appeared, then stroll out into the street. She was to walk directly to the hospital, as if she were going to visit "her grandfather."

"But when you get inside the hospital, hide in the gift shop," Nancy directed. "Bess and I will really call on Grandpa Soong and find out how he is. Wait for us to come back downstairs."

"Then after that," said George, "I'm to stroll on to Columbia University and walk around the campus. If somewhere along the line a suspicious person speaks to me or follows me, you two girls will do the rest."

"That's right," Nancy replied. "Let's go!"

Almost from the moment George appeared on the street, with Nancy and Bess following at a safe distance, people began to stare at the attractive "Chinese" girl. But no one stopped to speak to her or seemed to be following.

Nancy and Bess were beginning to think that perhaps their experiment was going to be a failure, when Bess suddenly grabbed her friend's arm. "Look at the man in that car!" she whispered tensely. "See how slowly he's going! And he's sure staring at George—I mean Chi Che."

The car, a dark-blue hardtop, was hugging the curb. The driver was about twenty-five years old.

He was slender and dark, but not an Oriental. He drove slowly as far as the hospital, watched "Chi Che" go in, then drove off.

"Do you think he might be connected with the case?" Bess asked Nancy.

"I don't know. We can't very well follow him, but I did get his license number."

The two girls walked into the hospital. They stopped at the desk to inquire the number of Mr. Soong's room, received passes to see him, then took the elevator upstairs.

The elderly man looked better and expressed his delight at seeing the callers. He said the doctor had told him he must remain in the hospital at least a week, maybe longer.

"Since I must stay here, I am asking you, Nancy, to bring my mail to me. And will you please answer my phone? There may be word from Chi Che. So far I have had none and do not know where to reach her."

"I'll be very happy to do that," Nancy answered.

Grandpa Soong told the girls that a nurse had brought him a message a short time before from Mr. Stromberg. He had telephoned to find out how the patient was.

"I have never met him," said the archaeologist, "so I consider it very kind that he has taken an interest in me."

Nancy and Bess wondered how the bookshop owner had learned of the attack on Mr. Soong.

Had someone at the apartment house told him?

On the bureau in the room stood a beautiful bouquet of yellow chrysanthemums. When Bess admired them, Grandpa Soong said, "I do not know who sent them. The card of good wishes which came with the flowers has no name on it."

"How strange!" Nancy remarked. "May I see the card?"

"Certainly. It is in the top drawer of the bureau."

As Nancy took out the card, she gave an involuntary start. In the lower right-hand corner was a hand-painted dragon! Printed on the card were the words: "Best wishes for a speedy recovery."

Nancy turned to Mr. Soong. "Surely you must have an idea who sent these?"

"Only a guess," he answered. "The person who gave my Chi Che the stationery may have heard of my illness and sent the flowers, but did not want me to feel obligated to write a note of thanks."

Nancy was glad that Grandpa Soong had no suspicions regarding the sender of the flowers. She herself was worried. The user of the dragon stationery obviously knew that Mr. Soong was in the hospital. Did this mean that the person had something to do with the attack?

Trying not to show her true feelings, the young sleuth said lightly, "Well, Grandpa Soong, you must have an unknown admirer. Isn't that exciting!"

She slipped the card back into the drawer and closed it.

"We must go now," she told Mr. Soong. "But we'll come again soon and make a longer visit."

"I shall look forward to seeing you. And I hope next time you will bring some letter or message from my Chi Che," Grandpa Soong added wistfully, handing Nancy the key to his lobby mailbox.

"Oh, something is bound to arrive," said Bess cheerfully. But as the girls walked down the hall to the elevator, she whispered to Nancy, "I wish I could have meant that. To tell the truth, I don't like the looks of things at all."

"It certainly is a puzzling situation," Nancy admitted. "Well, let's see what happens from here on."

"I'll tell you what may happen," Bess said. "If some of the Chinese students we met yesterday at Columbia see us and think Chi Che is with us, and then find out she's not Chi Che, it will give the whole thing away!"

Nancy agreed, and said that she and Bess would stay far enough behind George not to arouse any suspicion. When they reached the lobby, they walked into one door of the gift shop. George, seeing them, left by another. They followed a few seconds later.

When the girls reached the Columbia campus, George smiled at various students as they came

*Nancy and Bess stayed far enough behind George
not to arouse suspicion*

along. Suddenly she was thrilled to have someone wave to her from a distance and call out, "Good to see you back, Chi Che!"

Nancy and Bess had heard the remark. "The disguise is working!" Bess whispered excitedly.

As they went on, over a dozen young men and women students, some Oriental, others American, also waved and called to "Chi Che."

"Oh, isn't this exciting!" Bess exclaimed.

"Yes, but it doesn't seem to be leading us to the real Chi Che," Nancy replied.

The words were hardly out of her mouth when a young man, tall, red-haired, and very slender, rushed up to George. As he reached her he cried out, "How did you get away, Chi Che Soong? You little fool!"

Bess grabbed Nancy's arm. What was going to happen now?

George, though startled, played her role magnificently. She did not speak, merely shrugged her shoulders and extended the palms of both hands in a gesture of "You guess!"

The next instant the man seized George roughly by her arm and led her away. George pretended to go willingly. Nancy and Bess, with pounding hearts, kept pace with the two ahead.

CHAPTER VI

The Chase

WITH Nancy and Bess close on her heels, George was led by her captor from the campus and out to a side street. They were heading for a car parked at the curb. Its engine was running.

"That's the same car which was following George on the way to the hospital!" Nancy said, recognizing the license number.

"But there's a different driver!" Bess said.

As the masquerading "Chi Che" and her escort approached the car, the driver called out in a worried tone, "No take. While you were gone I phoned Ryle."

Startled, George's captor let go of her, jumped into the car, and it sped off.

Down the street Nancy saw an empty taxi. "Come on!" she cried to Bess, and ran to the cab. As Bess jumped in with her, Nancy called out to George, "Go home and wait for us." Then she ordered, "Driver, follow those two men who just left here!"

He started the taxi but seemed in no hurry to follow Nancy's order. Half turning in his seat, he asked, "What's going on here? You trying to date those guys?"

Nancy ignored the remark and merely said, "It's very important that we find out where they're going. Please hurry."

The driver shrugged and put on a little more speed. The chase took them onto the West Side Highway and downtown. As they reached the exit to Canal Street, the car ahead went down the ramp. The taxi followed.

By this time the suspicious driver of the fleeing car apparently had sensed that his car was being trailed. He made several turns, evidently trying to elude the pursuers.

"Those men may be going out to the end of Long Island," the taximan grumbled.

"It doesn't make any difference where they're going. I'd like you to keep them in view," Nancy said.

Bess sensed that the taxi driver was getting tired of the chase and probably was wondering whether he was going to get a tip large enough to warrant his trouble. Sweetly she said, "Driver, you're wonderful. I've never ridden with anyone who could handle a car so well."

The man beamed. "Thank you, miss. Not many people ever give me a compliment. They mostly complain." Now, eager to co-operate, he resumed the chase. As the taxi sped along Canal Street, suddenly the other car pulled up to the curb and stopped. The two men in it leaped out and ran at top speed down a side street.

"Now what?" the girls' taximan asked, stopping behind the other car.

"We'll go on foot from here," Nancy said.

She glanced at the meter, gave the driver the fare and a generous tip, then jumped from the taxi. She and Bess dashed up the street. The two men they had been following were not in sight.

"Why, we're in Chinatown, aren't we?" Bess exclaimed.

"That's right," Nancy agreed. "Those men probably don't live here, so it shouldn't be too hard to locate them. Somebody may be able to tell us where they are."

She and Bess went from shop to shop making inquiries, but no one had noticed the two running men. Finally Nancy was forced to admit defeat.

"Let's try something else," she told Bess. "We'll ask about the man called Ryle."

The girls inquired in the various stores and of people on the street if they knew anyone named Ryle. No one did.

"This is certainly disappointing," the young

sleuth remarked to Bess. "Well, our only chance of finding out who those men are is through the license plate of the car."

Nancy was determined not to give up her sleuthing completely. "But, at least, Bess, we can ask about Chi Che Soong," she added. "Let's try various places on Mott and Pell streets."

The girls decided to divide the task, with Bess taking one side of the street, Nancy the other. They had been at work on this project for nearly half an hour with no results, when Nancy came to a combination stationery, art, and knickknack store. Bess joined her.

"Remember the hand-painted dragon, Bess? I wonder if the owner of this shop might help us locate the place where the stationery and card were made?"

The girls walked in. First Nancy asked the Chinese shopkeeper if he knew Chi Che Soong. The man shook his head. "I am very sorry. May I help you in any other way?"

Nancy smiled. "Perhaps you can. I see you sell stationery. Have you ever seen any with a small hand-painted dragon in the lower right-hand corner?"

The shop owner opened a drawer and took out several sheets. "Is this what you mean?" he asked.

When Nancy said yes, the man smiled and told her he was the artist.

Nancy was excited by this information. "Do you

paint this stationery for some particular person?"

"No, no," the artist answered. "Many people, both Chinese and American, buy this stationery. I take no special orders. I will be glad to sell you some if you care to have any."

The young sleuth, thinking the unusual stationery might come in handy, bought a few sheets with envelopes to fit. "Do you also make cards with this design?" she asked.

Once more the man rummaged in the drawer. Presently he pulled out one exactly like the card which had been sent with Grandpa Soong's hospital flowers. Nancy said she would like to buy three or four.

"You don't make these on order either?" she asked.

The artist shook his head. Then he in turn asked, "Is there some special reason why you want to know?"

Nancy explained that a Chinese friend of hers had received a beautiful bouquet but that there was no name on the hand-painted dragon card. The recipient was most eager to find out who had sent the flowers.

"It's possible a man named Ryle is responsible," said Nancy. "Do you know anyone by that name?"

"Ryle?" the Chinese shopkeeper repeated. He looked into space for several seconds, then said, "A man named Ryle was in here several months ago with a friend. He did not buy any of this stationery or the cards. He was interested in selling me something."

"Oh, you also buy Oriental objects from people who come in here?" Nancy asked, to draw him out.

"Once in a while," the shop owner replied. "But in the case of Mr. Ryle, I must admit I refrained. He had some pieces of very fine jade with him. He said he had brought them from the Orient. I was afraid the jade might have been stolen or smuggled and I did not want to get into trouble."

Nancy's heart began to beat faster. Here indeed was an interesting clue!

But the young sleuth pretended to be shocked by the possibility that Mr. Ryle was a smuggler. "Then he can't be the man we have in mind," she said. "Do you know the first name of the Mr. Ryle who wanted to sell you the jade?"

"No, I didn't hear it," the man answered. "The only reason I know his name is Ryle is because his companion called him that. The men haven't been in here since, so I know nothing more about them."

"This man named Ryle—was he stout?" Bess queried, hoping to get more information for Nancy.

"No. In fact, he was a small, slender man. But he looked very strong," the stationer replied. A customer came in just then, so Nancy and Bess took their leave. Out on the street once more, the girl detective said, "I think we've hit upon a real clue. This small, slender but muscular man we keep hearing about must be named Ryle! But is Ryle his first or last name?"

"Good question," Bess remarked. "And how do you spell it?"

The girls walked back to Canal Street to hail a taxi. To their amazement the car in which the two suspects had driven to Chinatown was still standing there.

"I think I'll phone the police about this," Nancy told Bess.

She went into a drugstore and called Captain Gray. Without revealing anything about the mystery surrounding Chi Che, Nancy said she had picked up a clue which might lead to the man who had attacked Grandpa Soong. She mentioned the parked car and its license number.

"I'll look into the matter at once," the officer promised.

Nancy had a hunch that the car had been abandoned, so there was little point in waiting for the two men to return. She signaled a taxi and directed the driver to take her and Bess back to Aunt Eloise's apartment.

Meanwhile, George had been having an adventure of her own. Right after Nancy and Bess had driven off in the taxi, a Chinese girl, carrying an armful of books, had rushed up to her. She had spoken excitedly in what George assumed was Cantonese, but the only words George could distinguish were "Chi Che." Did the girl think she was Chi Che or had she seen through her disguise?

Suddenly the Chinese girl, frowning, looked more closely at George. Then she laughed and in English apologized. "Oh, I thought you were a girl I know named Chi Che Soong. My, how much you look like her! I stopped you because I heard Chi Che left her job at Stromberg's Bookshop. I wondered if I could get it."

George Fayne took an instant liking to the attractive Chinese girl. The stranger introduced herself as Lily Alys Wu. After a little more conversation, George had an idea.

"Perhaps I can get the job for you at the bookshop," she said. "Would you like to talk it over?"

"Yes. But first, please explain why you are costumed and made up the way you are. You see, I am one of Chi Che's closest friends."

George smiled but did not reply at once. Could she trust Lily Alys with confidential information about the missing Chi Che?

CHAPTER VII

Strange Thefts

As GEORGE stood debating whether or not to tell Lily Alys Wu about Chi Che, an elderly gentleman carrying a brief case came along the street. He and the Chinese girl smiled at each other.

"How are you, Professor Rankin?" Lily said.

"Very well, thank you, Miss Wu. And you?"

"Fine. I certainly enjoyed your lecture yesterday."

"I am glad," Professor Rankin said, and tipping his hat, went on his way.

The little episode helped George make up her mind. She was sure she could trust Lily Alys.

"The reason I'm masquerading as your friend Chi Che Soong," she said, "is because Chi Che seems to be missing."

"Missing!" Lily exclaimed. "I know she hasn't been to classes for the past few days. I was going to phone her this afternoon. Please tell me more."

George was guarded in her statements, but did reveal that Mr. Soong had not heard from his granddaughter since she left a note saying she planned to visit some college friends. "Did you know Mr. Soong is in the hospital?" George asked.

"No," Lily Alys replied. "I am so sorry to hear that. What is the trouble?"

Since the story had appeared in the newspapers, George told what had happened to the elderly man.

"That is dreadful!" Lily Alys said. "I am very fond of Mr. Soong. And I know Chi Che loves and respects him very much. I cannot understand why she would stay away and not communicate with him."

"That is what my friends and I cannot understand, either," said George. "Would you be willing to come to the apartment where we're staying and discuss the situation? Perhaps you can give us some clue to where Chi Che might be."

Lily Alys said she would be happy to come. The two girls walked along side by side. There was no further recognition of "Chi Che" by any passers-by.

When they reached the apartment, Aunt Eloise, who had just arrived, opened the door for them. Since Nancy and Bess were not there yet, the conversation was general. Aunt Eloise served tea and cookies.

Presently Nancy and Bess announced themselves over the speaking tube at the front door and a few minutes later entered the apartment.

George introduced Lily Alys Wu and explained why she had brought the Chinese girl to call. Then, on a pretext that she had something in her purse to give Nancy, George asked her to come into the bedroom a moment.

Quickly the two girls exchanged stories. Then George propounded the idea she had had for the past half hour; that Lily Alys, who, like Chi Che, was a linguist, try for a position at Stromberg's Bookshop.

Nancy smiled. "I think I know what you have in mind, George. You suspect that Chi Che's message to Aunt Eloise might have meant she had found out some secret about the bookshop, and perhaps Lily Alys can learn the same thing without being caught."

"Exactly," said George. "And I feel sure Lily Alys can be trusted."

Nancy too was certain of this. She and George returned to the living room and broached the subject to the Chinese girl. "That is, if you're fortunate enough to get the position at the bookshop," George added.

Lily Alys screwed up her face and looked a little frightened at the idea. "I do not know that I am capable of such work," she said. "I have never had anything to do with solving mysteries."

"It won't be hard," George urged her. "Just do

the jobs Mr. Stromberg asks you to, but keep your eyes and ears open."

"And pay special attention to telephone calls," Nancy added.

The young Chinese student finally agreed and said that she hoped she would not fail in her assignment.

"I will go over to Mr. Stromberg's at once," Lily promised, "and let you know later whether or not I succeed in obtaining the position."

Nancy went to the door with their new friend, and the others called, "Good luck!"

As soon as Lily Alys had left, Nancy telephoned police headquarters. There was no news about the identity of Mr. Soong's attacker, the sergeant on duty reported. "The car the suspects were riding in," he added, "was found to have been stolen."

As Nancy thanked him and hung up, she shrugged resignedly. "Another clue has faded out," she told her friends.

George went into her bedroom to change her clothes and remove the Chinese make-up. Suddenly she called out, "Did one of you knock my clock onto the floor?"

"No," the others chorused.

"Then someone was in here while we were all away!" George exclaimed.

When they heard this, everyone rushed into the bedroom. George pointed to her traveling clock which lay on the floor by the bed.

"But how could anyone get in here?" Aunt Eloise asked.

Nancy and Bess looked at each other sheepishly. They had forgotten to lock the door between the Soong apartment and Aunt Eloise's!

"Evidently the person who has the key to the Soongs' let himself in and came through," Nancy said.

Instantly a search was begun, but twenty minutes later Aunt Eloise declared that apparently nothing had been taken.

"Then why was he in here?" George demanded.

No one could answer her question. But suddenly Bess gasped. "Maybe the intruder was hiding in the Soong apartment while Lily Alys was here and overheard our plan!"

Nancy, although concerned, pointed out that this was not necessarily true. The clock, probably knocked to the floor by the intruder, had stopped hours before. "I don't think the person would have stayed around all this time."

"I hope you're right." Bess sighed.

Nancy was quiet for a full minute, then she said, "Perhaps the intruder was hunting for Chi Che's note to Grandpa Soong. When he didn't find it in their apartment, he may have figured it was in here."

"And it was!" said Bess. "Where is it now?"

Nancy rushed to a desk and pulled open the

top drawer. "Gone!" she cried. "I put it in here with Chi Che's photograph. In fact, that's gone too."

"Oh, dear, what's going to happen now?" Bess worried.

Again Nancy was silent for a while. Then she said, "It's my guess that the person who came in here wanted a sample of Chi Che's Chinese handwriting. I believe Grandpa Soong will be receiving a new note. It will be a forgery imitating Chi Che's writing."

"And what do you think it will say?" Aunt Eloise asked.

"It will beg Grandpa Soong not to notify the police of her absence."

Nancy telephoned police headquarters to report the latest theft. Two plain-clothes men arrived a short while later. After making a routine investigation, they said they had found nothing significant and went off.

A few minutes later Aunt Eloise produced a paper bag. "I stopped at a hardware store on my way home," she told the girls. "I decided that if one more intruder came into either apartment, I was going to put bolts on the hall doors. Who wants to help me play carpenter?"

Bess said, "I'll be glad to help. But suppose Chi Che should return and can't get in?"

Aunt Eloise said she felt certain now that Chi

Che was not going to return until she was found by Detective Nancy Drew and her friends or by the police. "However, I'll tell the superintendent I've bolted the doors. If Chi Che should come back and not be able to get in, I'm sure she'll go to him and he'll explain."

Suddenly Nancy laughed. "We can barricade the Soongs' apartment," she said, "but we'd have to use a little magic to bolt ours after we've left it!"

Aunt Eloise blinked and laughed. "Why, of course," she said. "I was certainly letting my imagination run away with me."

Nancy added that it would be a good idea to barricade the Soongs' apartment, nevertheless. "I'm positive that the intruder won't return here since he found what he wanted—the photograph and the letter."

She and her aunt attached the bolt to the Soongs' living-room hall door. Then it was shot into place and the connecting door between the two apartments also bolted.

"Anybody hungry?" the teacher asked as she and Nancy joined Bess and George.

"I'm starved!" Bess answered quickly.

The other girls smiled. It seemed that Bess, who rarely watched her weight, could eat at any time!

"I have a casserole dish in the refrigerator, ready to slip into the oven," Aunt Eloise said. "I hope you'll all like it."

The four entered the kitchen. Miss Drew turned on the automatic pilot to light the oven. Then she turned and started to walk toward the refrigerator.

Suddenly there was an explosion inside the stove. The oven door flew off, hitting Aunt Eloise squarely in the back and knocking her over!

CHAPTER VIII

Angry Neighbors

FEARFUL that there might possibly be a second explosion, Nancy and George lifted Aunt Eloise and rushed from the kitchen. They laid the teacher gently on her bed.

"Aunt Eloise," Nancy said, trying not to show her fright, "are you hurt?"

Her aunt smiled wanly. "I only had the wind knocked out of me, I guess," she said.

The girls were greatly relieved, but Nancy felt that she should investigate. She wondered if the explosion might have been caused by an accumulation of leaking gas. "It could've been ignited when the pilot was turned on, but we would have smelled the escaping gas when we were in the living room," Nancy said to herself.

Puzzled, she entered the kitchen and walked to the stove. She gazed into the doorless oven.

There were tiny bits of red paper and particles of sand lying about.

"Someone planted another giant firecracker! So that's what the intruder was doing in here, as well as taking Chi Che's photograph and letter."

The young sleuth went back to report to her aunt and the girls.

"How perfectly dreadful!" Bess exclaimed. "In solving a mystery it's bad enough to go after an enemy, but when he invades your home to k-kill you, maybe, it's pretty awful!"

"I'm sure he didn't mean to go that far, but he *is* trying to scare me into giving up the case," Nancy remarked.

Suddenly someone began to pound on the hall door. Nancy went to find out who it was. Several people stood there. They announced they were neighbors, on the same floor.

"What's going on here?" demanded a very stout, red-faced man.

"We—er—had a little accident with our stove," Nancy answered, thinking it best not to tell him the whole story.

"Is that all?" the man prodded.

"Come see for yourself," Nancy said. She was sure he would never guess the truth even if he noticed the bits of red paper and sand.

The whole group of neighbors crowded into the apartment and went to the kitchen. "Door blew off, eh?" the red-faced man remarked. "Well, you ought to be more careful how you use gas."

Apparently he was satisfied with Nancy's explanation. But a sharp-faced, thin woman in the group said accusingly, "Something strange is going on, and it has to do with those Soongs. And you seem to be pretty friendly with that queer old man."

"He's not queer," Nancy defended the archaeologist. "He's a very learned and fine person."

"Maybe so," the woman admitted. "Just the same, I don't like living in a place where firecrackers are going off and people are getting knocked out by intruders."

George, who had appeared in the doorway by this time, could not refrain from commenting, "Then perhaps you should move?"

The woman glared at her. *"Me* move?" she cried out. "I think the Soongs and Miss Drew should be the ones to go. You're—you're all dangerous tenants!"

Nancy remarked icily, "Instead of you people becoming so angry and unfriendly, I think you should welcome the chance to help the police capture the person who is responsible for harming Grandpa Soong."

"What do you mean?" asked a small, shy woman.

The young sleuth told her that if any of the neighbors had seen a suspicious person in the hallway or on the elevator, he should report it now. There was dead silence for several seconds as the men and women looked at one another. Then finally the shy little woman spoke up.

"I've been so scared since that firecracker went off in the hall, I've hesitated to say anything. But I think Miss Drew's niece is right. I may have a clue. Early this afternoon I was about to go shopping. As I have been doing, I opened my door a crack and looked out to see if anyone was in the hall. I saw a short, slender man sneaking along from the stairway toward the Soongs' apartment. I was so frightened I closed my door, so I really don't know where he went."

"What time was this?" Nancy asked her.

"About three o'clock."

Nancy's thoughts began to race. The short, slender man could be the same one whom she herself had seen in the apartment hallway before the first firecracker went off. He might even have been the man driving the car which had followed George to the hospital when she played the part of Chi Che! He would have had time to change drivers, come to the Soong apartment, let himself in with the key stolen from Chi Che, and plant the firecracker in Miss Drew's stove!

The outspoken woman apologized for what she had said, and promised to be alert for any suspicious persons and report them to the superintendent or to the police. The group disbanded and Nancy closed the door.

Aunt Eloise declared she was feeling better and

she and the girls discussed the affair. "One thing is sure," George spoke up. "Several people are trying to scare us off the case."

"And in *my* case," said Bess, "they're almost succeeding. Maybe we should give up the entire thing."

Aunt Eloise said she, for one, would not do this. She felt obligated to the Soongs to keep trying to solve the mystery of Chi Che's disappearance.

"And I'm certainly going to stick by you," Nancy determined. "But there is something I think we should do: take Police Captain Gray into our confidence." Her aunt agreed.

Nancy called the officer, who promised to come to the apartment that evening. After she reported this to the others, Nancy said:

"Tonight I'm going to treat everybody to supper at a nice restaurant. I think Aunt Eloise has seen enough of her kitchen for today."

Although Miss Drew objected, she finally admitted that she would enjoy going out to eat. Bess and George accepted readily. The foursome had a delightful meal at a small French restaurant famous for its excellent cuisine.

Soon after the group had returned to the apartment, Police Captain Gray arrived. He listened intently as Nancy related the whole story from the discovery of Chi Che's note addressed to Eloise Drew to the recent explosion.

"Nancy Drew, I'm intrigued by your sleuthing ability," he said, smiling. "I couldn't have had a better report from one of my top men."

Captain Gray said that he would have the apartment house, as well as the Drew and Soong apartments, watched twenty-four hours a day. "All visitors will be checked."

The officer, as Nancy had requested, promised not to give out the story of Chi Che's disappearance, except to the particular police who would be assigned to the case. "I agree with you that it might endanger her life," he said.

Just as Captain Gray was leaving, the telephone rang. Miss Drew answered it, then called Nancy. "Please wait," she requested the captain.

"This is Lily Alys," the caller said. "Nancy, I got the job at the bookshop!"

"Good!" Nancy replied. "I'll probably see you there. But, Lily Alys, if I should come to the shop, or Bess or George, act as if you had never seen us before."

"All right," the Chinese girl promised. "And I'll try hard to do some detecting for you."

Nancy reported the conversation to the officer, then he left. Before the young sleuth retired she told the others she was going to call on Grandpa Soong the following day. "I'll take any mail that has come. And if there's one signed Chi Che, I'm sure it will be a fake. She would never stay away if she knew her grandfather were ill."

The next morning Aunt Eloise and the girls attended church. Then at about two o'clock Nancy suddenly remembered her promise to check Mr. Soong's mail and went to the vestibule. There were three letters for the elderly man in the box. One was an advertisement. Another, in a man's handwriting, was postmarked Hong Kong. The third had been addressed by a woman, Nancy felt sure. It was stamped special delivery and was postmarked New Haven, Connecticut.

"This one might be from Chi Che! The writing is similar," Nancy thought excitedly, and hurried on to the hospital.

She found Grandpa Soong feeling better, but sad and puzzled about his granddaughter. "I have had no word from Chi Che," he said.

"I think I have a letter for you from her," Nancy remarked cheerfully, and handed over the mail.

"This is indeed from my Chi Che!" the elderly man exclaimed. "You will forgive me if I read it."

With trembling fingers Grandpa Soong opened the envelope and took out a sheet of stationery. From where Nancy had seated herself, she could see that the letter was written in Chinese characters. And in the lower right-hand corner was a fire dragon!

A smile came over Grandpa Soong's face. "Chi Che's friends are taking her on a long trip. She says I am not to worry."

"Well, that is reassuring," Nancy said with a smile. But inwardly she was more worried than ever. Surely Chi Che would not of her own volition have notified her grandfather of such plans by letter instead of telephoning him. Nancy was fearful that Chi Che had been abducted, and perhaps taken out of the country!

"I wonder how long Chi Che will be gone," Grandpa Soong mused. "Well, I must be patient. I will work hard on the foreword of my book and help to pass the time," he said sadly.

The elderly man asked if the police had any clues to the person who had stolen his manuscript. Nancy had to admit that they had turned up none yet, but were working hard on the case.

"Grandpa Soong," she said, "you may think me very rude, but I should like very much to have this letter from Chi Che. If I bring it back soon, may I borrow it?"

The archaeologist did not even ask her why she wanted the note. "Take it, my dear. And there is no hurry about your bringing it back."

The next morning Nancy went directly to Columbia University and talked to the young woman assistant in the dean's office who had been so helpful before. Nancy obtained samples of Chi Che's handwriting, not only in English, but also in Chinese.

"Any news of when Chi Che may return?" the assistant asked.

"We do not know," Nancy replied. "I suppose you are curious why I want the samples of Chi Che's writing. The reason is that her grandfather received a letter from her which I suspect is a forgery. I'd like to determine if it is. But please say nothing about this to anyone."

Nancy left the young woman staring in amazement after her. She hurried directly to Captain Gray's office and showed him both the envelope and the fire-dragon stationery with its message.

"I suspect this may be a forgery," she told the officer. "Could you possibly have a handwriting expert analyze it?"

"Yes, at once," Captain Gray agreed. "This may be an invaluable clue."

Nancy also confided her fear that Chi Che might have been taken from the country. The captain frowned, and said he would notify the FBI. He then suggested that Nancy return to headquarters in about two hours. The young detective thanked him and left, but she was back soon after lunch.

"Nancy Drew, you have scored another bull's-eye," the officer told her. "The note in Chinese and the envelope in English received today by Mr. Soong are definitely the work of a forger."

"Can you tell me any more?" Nancy asked.

"Yes, several things. Most important, perhaps, is that this note and envelope were written by a woman!"

CHAPTER IX

Bess Is Missing

"A woman!" Nancy exclaimed. "I wonder who she is—probably the wife of one of the men involved in the case."

"No doubt," said Captain Gray.

"Will you show me some of the differences in the two handwritings, so that if I come across the fake one again, I might be able to spot the forger?"

"Be glad to, Nancy." Captain Gray laid the envelope of the letter which had just come to Mr. Soong and the sample of Chi Che's handwriting in English, side by side.

"One of the hardest things to imitate in handwriting is the crossing of t's," the officer explained. "The forger is trying to be so careful that he usually goes slower and the line is slightly more wavy than the original writer would make it. Look at these two through this magnifying glass.

"The letter 'y' is another interesting one to

look for," Captain Gray stated. "If it is an unfinished one with the tail going straight down, it is apt to be off center or wobbly. If it's a completed 'y,' it's even easier to spot."

Nancy studied the y's on the two different samples of writing. "It's very evident," she said. "This is fascinating." Then her brow furrowed. "Captain Gray, do you agree that Chi Che is being held against her will?"

"I would say yes," the officer answered. "Furthermore, she probably was taken away somewhere else before any members of the gang even thought of sending this note. For that reason, they had to forge it."

"Shall I take this letter back to Mr. Soong?" the young detective asked. "He may become suspicious, and that's what we're trying to avoid."

The officer nodded. "We have made good photostats of it. Take the letter back, but suggest to Mr. Soong that it might be accidentally thrown away in the hospital and would be safer with you. Then suppose you return it to me."

Nancy smiled understandingly and left. She found Grandpa Soong sitting up in bed, writing. He did not object to her suggestion about the letter, so she took it back to police headquarters.

"I think I'll drop in at Stromberg's Bookshop and see how Lily Alys is making out," Nancy told Captain Gray. "Perhaps she has picked up a clue already!"

Nancy hurried to the shop. There were several customers who were being assisted by both Mr. Stromberg and Lily Alys. Nancy gave no sign of recognizing the Chinese girl who presently came up to her and asked:

"May I help you?"

"Yes," Nancy replied. "I'm looking for a book on the geology of New York State. Do you happen to have one in stock?"

"I think we have," Lily Alys said. "Will you come over this way, please?"

The young clerk found the volume. "Is there something else?" she asked sweetly.

"I'm not sure." Nancy looked around. "The shop is fascinating. I'd like to browse a little."

"Very well," Lily Alys said. "Let me know if you find anything else you wish to buy."

In an undertone which no one else in the shop could hear, the Chinese girl said quickly, "On the third shelf of the travel books is a volume about Asia which contains an article on Hong Kong. Inside the book I found a piece of dragon stationery."

"Was there anything written on it?" Nancy asked.

"The paper looked blank on both sides. But maybe *you* can find something."

Quickly Lily Alys went over to the desk, made out a sales slip for the book on geology, then went up to another customer. In the meantime,

Nancy wandered around glancing at various volumes. Finally she came to the travel section and found the book which Lily Alys had mentioned.

She took it from the shelf, and began to look through the volume. Presently she came to a chapter on Hong Kong. But there was no piece of stationery among the leaves!

"Someone has taken it out," Nancy thought. "I wonder who. Mr. Stromberg? Or someone who is using the bookshop to leave or collect secret messages? Or maybe the sheet was only a mark to indicate something in the chapter," she deduced. "I think I'll buy this book."

She walked back toward the desk with it and told Lily Alys that she would purchase the book about Asia as well as the other. As Nancy said this, Mr. Stromberg abruptly left the customer on whom he was waiting and rushed to Nancy's side.

"That book is not for sale!" he informed her in a sharp tone of voice.

Nancy looked at the man in amazement. "Not for sale?" she repeated. "It was on the shelf."

"Nevertheless, that volume is not for sale!" Mr. Stromberg cried excitedly. "Give it to me!" Without waiting for her to do so, he snatched it from her hand.

Nancy pretended to be shocked by his action. "Why, is something the matter with the book?"

"Yes—uh—it's out of date. You'll have to wait until the revised edition is published."

"Oh, I don't mind if it's old," said Nancy disarmingly. "I love to read about Asia."

By this time Mr. Stromberg's face was red with anger and he once more vehemently refused to sell the book. Nancy was sure now that the book held some clue to the mystery of the fire dragon. The question was how much did Mr. Stromberg know about it? Was he shielding someone else? Had he been asked not to sell the volume and had it inadvertently been put on the shelf?

Nancy shrugged. "If you won't sell it, you won't sell it," she said. "Well, I'll just pay for the other book I bought."

Mr. Stromberg accompanied Nancy to the desk. He wrapped the book on geology himself and took her money. There was no chance for Lily Alys to tell Nancy any more, but the young sleuth was determined to find out later that day if the Chinese girl had come across additional information.

As Nancy walked along the street toward Aunt Eloise's apartment, she decided to try another bookshop for a copy of the book on Asia. She found one without any trouble, then hurried home.

"Hello, everybody," Nancy called, entering the apartment. Seeing only Aunt Eloise and George in the living room, she asked, "Where's Bess?"

"She went marketing for me," Miss Drew replied.

"That book is not for sale!" he informed Nancy

Nancy told about her experience in the bookshop and the others agreed that something strange was going on there. Next, Nancy turned to the chapter on Hong Kong in the book on Asia. First came the history of the city, then suggestions to tourists on what to see, and finally a list of shops known for fine jewelry, linen, furniture, and clothing of all kinds.

"Hong Kong is the place for expert tailoring and dressmaking," Nancy remarked. "My, and listen to these prices. Things cost about one third what they do in this country!"

"Me for Hong Kong." George chuckled, taking the book. Presently she said, "There doesn't seem to be anything out of the ordinary in this chapter. Maybe the contents of the book had nothing to do with the piece of dragon stationery inside."

"Then why wouldn't Mr. Stromberg have sold me his copy?" Nancy argued. "I think perhaps some phrase or sentence was underlined and he didn't want anybody to see it."

George suggested that perhaps they should have the police keep a watch on Mr. Stromberg. Aunt Eloise shook her head. "He might be innocent of anything underhanded. A customer may have asked him to reserve that particular volume, and not being a very diplomatic person, he practically lost his head because Nancy wanted to purchase it."

Nancy said that as soon as Lily Alys was back in her dormitory at Columbia she was going to phone her. She looked at her watch. "By the way, how long has Bess been gone?"

"Too long," Aunt Eloise replied. "She should have been back an hour ago. I can't understand it."

Nancy was concerned too. "Perhaps we should go out and try to find her."

At that moment the telephone rang. It was Lily Alys. "Oh, Nancy, I've lost my job!" the Chinese girl said worriedly.

"I'm not surprised," Nancy told her. "And I'm sure it's all my fault. Mr. Stromberg became suspicious after the book episode. Isn't that it?"

"Yes, partly," Lily Alys replied. "After all the customers had gone, he called me to the desk and handed me a few dollars. He looked at me hard and said, 'Young lady, I don't know what your game is, but I want a clerk I can trust—not someone that brings customers in here to cause a scene.'"

"He meant me!" Nancy exclaimed. "I believe that Mr. Stromberg must suspect you and I know each other."

"I'm afraid so," said Lily Alys.

Nancy asked if the Chinese girl had had a chance to look at the pages between which she had found the piece of fire-dragon stationery.

"Yes, I did. In the list of shops it mentioned 'mah-jongg sets.' Those two words were underlined."

"That might be a clue," Nancy said. "Did anything else happen to cause Mr. Stromberg to discharge you?"

Lily Alys gave a great sigh. "Just before that happened, he went into his office in the back. I wanted to ask him a question, so walked to the door. I was just in time to hear him say on the phone 'Don't use books again to get your message across.'"

The Chinese girl said she felt sure that Mr. Stromberg knew she had heard him and this actually was the reason he had discharged her. "Oh, I am sorry I failed in my mission," Lily Alys added woefully.

"Please don't worry about it," said Nancy. "You've been a big help. Besides, I'm sure you can find a safer position somewhere else with no detective work to do."

Lily Alys agreed. "But I had hoped to do more to help find Chi Che," she said.

"You may learn something yet," Nancy told her. "If you do, be sure to let me know."

Lily Alys promised to do so, then hung up. Nancy told Aunt Eloise and George what she had just learned, then went back to the book and began to look for shops selling mah-jongg sets. There were several, and since Lily Alys had not mentioned the name of any shop, the young sleuth suggested that Lily hardly had a chance to notice the name. "She probably had to close the book in a hurry, before Mr. Stromberg saw her looking in it," Nancy surmised.

"But I'll bet anything he did," George said.

Aunt Eloise, who had been gazing out the window, said worriedly, "I'm really becoming frantic about Bess. I can't imagine why she's staying away so long. She told me she would come directly home, since some of the groceries were needed for supper tonight."

Nancy urged that she and George delay no longer in trying to locate Bess. They got a list from Aunt Eloise of the three stores to which Bess intended to go, then set out. At the first two stores they learned nothing, but the cashier at the third one, a large market, said she remembered pretty, blond-haired Bess.

"That girl was loaded down with bundles," she told Nancy and George. "She and a woman behind her were laughing and talking about going in the woman's car to help the girl get all her packages home."

"Have you any idea who this woman was?" Nancy asked quickly.

"No, I haven't," the cashier answered. "I had never seen her before tonight."

George and Nancy went out to the street, trying to guess where Bess could have gone.

"Frankly, George, I'm terribly worried," Nancy said. "That woman who offered to give Bess a ride may be part of the gang that's holding Chi Che. The woman could even be the forger of the letter to Grandpa Soong!"

"Oh, Nancy, I hope you're wrong!" George said fervently. "We'd better report Bess's disappearance to Captain Gray."

But Nancy was not wrong. At that very moment Bess was seated on a chair, her eyes blindfolded and her hands tied behind her back. She had no idea where she was.

Bess's heart pounded in fright. She berated herself, "Oh, what a fool I was to get into this mess!"

Her mind raced over events of the past hours. First she had encountered the pleasant woman with Eurasian features in the supermarket. The woman had said that she was a good friend of Miss Eloise Drew, and had offered to drive Bess and her many bundles to the apartment house.

Bess had accepted and the two had gone out to the car. Behind the wheel was a man who, the woman said, was her husband. Bess had noted only that he had red hair.

The moment they had climbed into the rear of the car, the woman had dropped her purse on the floor. Bess had leaned over to pick it up. The next instant she had been pushed down to the floor and warned to keep still or she would be sorry.

Now, Bess thought desperately, she was a prisoner in some unknown place. Was the red-haired man the same one who had taken George from the Columbia campus? The Eurasian woman, who was far from pleasant now, was saying harshly:

"You'd better tell us what your pal Nancy Drew is up to! And you don't leave here until you do!"

CHAPTER X

Bookshop Detectives

BESS MARVIN sat in speechless amazement as her two captors continued to quiz her about Nancy's sleuthing. How had they learned she was working on the case?

"If you won't talk," the woman warned in a harsh voice, "you may never see her again!"

Bess was terrified, for she feared these people might carry out their threat. Yet she did not intend to give away any of Nancy's plans for solving the mystery.

Two rough hands gripped Bess's shoulders and shook her. She was sure they belonged to the red-haired man.

"Listen here," he said, "this silence won't do you any good. If *you* won't tell us what's going on, we'll get hold of that interfering young detective herself!"

All this time Bess had been desperately racking her brain for a likely story to allay the suspicions of her captors. Suddenly an inspiration came to her.

"Take your hands off me!" Bess ordered. "I'll tell you why Nancy Drew is in New York."

"Well, it's about time," the woman said unpleasantly. "Talk and be sure it's the truth!"

Bess explained that Mr. Drew was a lawyer and his law cases took him to many places. Nancy often did research for her father in order to save him time.

"Mr. Drew is planning a trip to Hong Kong," Bess went on. "He thought if Nancy talked to some people who had been there, and read some good books on the subject, it would be of assistance to him. Mr. Drew's case concerns a will."

There was a long silence, then Bess could hear the couple whispering. The imprisoned girl waited in an agony of suspense. Had her explanation been convincing enough? Would they let her go?

In a few minutes the woman spoke. "We're going to let you go. But not until after dark and not until we get you far away from this place. We don't want you to know where you've been so you can inform the police."

"Yeah," said the man. "You'd better not tell the police or anybody else *anything,* if you know what's good for you!"

A little later Bess was ordered to get up and walk. The woman held her by one arm, the man by the other. Presently she sensed that they had entered an elevator. She felt the descent, then Bess knew she was being led outdoors. She was shoved into a car and made to sit on the floor.

The motor was already running and the car started off at once. The drive was a long one, and so jolting that Bess was continually bumping her face against the hard seats. She felt that she was surely coming out of this adventure with a black-and-blue nose!

Finally, to her relief, the automobile was stopped. The couple helped Bess out and walked her a short distance.

"Don't move or you'll get run over," the woman warned her. "Somebody will come along and find you. And remember, don't go to the police."

"Come on!" the man barked.

Bess heard the car door slam and the automobile roar away.

"Oh, where am I?" Bess wondered, thankful to be free, but feeling utterly helpless.

From the freshness of the air and relative lack of traffic noise she figured she was out of the city. She could hear cars not too far away, but apparently none of the drivers saw her. Though Bess had been warned not to move, she did lean over and manage to feel the ground. Dirt and grass!

"I'm at the side of some road," she thought, straightening up again.

At that instant Bess heard an oncoming car, then a screech of brakes. A moment later a car door opened and someone took off the blindfold. Her rescuer was an elderly man, and in the car sat a white-haired woman.

"Oh, thank you, sir," Bess gasped in relief. "Please untie my hands, too."

The man gave a grunt. "They carry these hazings too far!" he said. "What the fraternity boys do is bad enough, but when the sorority girls get to tying new members up and leaving them by the road after dark, it's going beyond all sense!"

"It certainly is," the woman agreed.

Bess smiled wanly. She said nothing—unwittingly the elderly couple had supplied her with an explanation that satisfied them.

The man helped Bess into the rear seat of his sedan, and inquired where she would like to be dropped. "At your sorority house?" he asked.

"I think not," said Bess. "I'd like to go home. Are you going into New York City?"

"Yes, we are," the man replied. "I'll be glad to take you home."

"You are most kind, but just drop me anywhere in the city."

The couple, however, insisted upon driving Bess to her home. Finally she directed them to the apartment house where Aunt Eloise lived. In Bess's purse was a small bottle of a lovely French perfume she had purchased that day. As she opened the door to step from the car, she handed the package to the woman.

"Please take this and enjoy it. You have no idea how grateful I am to you." She hurried across the sidewalk before the woman could comment.

When Bess rang the outer doorbell and announced she was home, she could hear shrieks of delight from the apartment. The inner door clicked open and she hurried to the elevator. Aunt Eloise and the other girls hugged her joyfully, demanding to know where she had been.

"I'm not supposed to tell you," Bess said. Now that her great fright was over, she could not help teasing the others.

"If you don't," threatened her cousin George, "*we* won't tell you what we found out this afternoon."

Bess made a face, then told her story. The others were aghast and Aunt Eloise insisted that despite the warning of Bess's captors, they should tell Captain Gray the whole story.

"I suppose he'll want me to look through the rogues' gallery to see if I can find that woman." Bess sighed wearily. "Well, please ask him to make it tomorrow. I'm starving and I certainly will be glad to tumble into my bed."

As Aunt Eloise went to telephone the police captain, Nancy and George hurried to the kitchen. They prepared an appetizing meal for Bess and sat down with her while she ate. Then she went directly to bed and the others soon followed.

At breakfast the next morning the whole subject was discussed again. As Bess suspected, Captain Gray had requested her to come to headquarters and try to pick out the woman in the rogues' gallery. George offered to go with her.

"Maybe I can spot the red-haired man," she said. The two girls left after the meal was finished.

As Nancy helped her aunt get ready for school, she said, "I'd like to try a little sleuthing from a different angle. I am more and more convinced that Stromberg's Bookshop is a front for an underhanded scheme. Could you ask some friend of yours to go there and find out if Mr. Stromberg has a new clerk?"

"I could ask my friend Mrs. Becker."

"I'd like her to do something else, too," said Nancy. "Do you think she would ask Mr. Stromberg to come to her home and look at some foreign books she'll say she wants to sell? I'll get the volumes for her."

"Certainly," said Aunt Eloise. "I'll call her right now." She smiled. "I suppose while he's gone, you'll go to the shop to look around again." Her niece nodded.

Miss Drew dialed the number. Then, since it was getting late, she introduced her niece to Mrs. Becker and told the two to continue the conversation. Nancy waved good-by to her aunt, then explained her request to Mrs. Becker.

"To avoid suspicion that I'm involved in this plan," Nancy said, "I'll have the books delivered to your home instead of bringing them myself."

Mrs. Becker promised that as soon as the books arrived, she would look them over carefully so that she would know the contents. "Then I'll go to Stromberg's Bookshop and talk to the owner. If he agrees to come to my apartment, I'll let you know what time it will be."

Nancy thanked her, then hurried off to the bookstore near the university where she had purchased her copy of the Asian book. She bought several foreign volumes in various languages. All of them were old, first editions, and rather hard to obtain, according to the bookshop owner. This was exactly what Nancy had wanted!

"Could you deliver this package immediately?" she asked the owner. The man said yes. After the books were wrapped, Nancy carefully wrote Mrs. Becker's name and address on the package, paid for all the books, then left the store.

By the time Nancy returned to the apartment, Bess and George were back. "I wasn't able to identify any photograph in the rogues' gallery," Bess said.

"And I didn't find the red-haired man," George added.

"They must be new at their racket," Nancy remarked.

She told the cousins of her plan for sleuthing. "I thought you girls and I would go to Stromberg's Bookshop while Mr. Stromberg's at Mrs.

Becker's. You stand guard in the front room, while I take a look in that back room!"

The three girls had just finished their luncheon when Mrs. Becker telephoned. The woman said she had gone over to the shop during the morning but learned little. Mr. Stromberg was most solicitous in helping her pick out a book she planned to buy. There was a new young woman clerk, not too efficient, assisting.

"Mr. Stromberg is coming to my apartment at two o'clock this afternoon," Mrs. Becker told Nancy.

"Oh, that's fine," the young sleuth said. "And thank you for your help, Mrs. Becker."

At exactly two o'clock Nancy, Bess, and George arrived at Mr. Stromberg's shop. As prearranged, the girls took up their positions. Bess at once began chatting with the clerk, and took her to a front corner of the shop where the books on fashion designing and dressmaking were located. It was easy for Bess to keep the young woman intrigued by her chatter on the subject of clothes.

George wandered around the shop, trying to pick up any clues which they might have overlooked before. Nancy, meanwhile, had slipped into the back room when the clerk was not looking. She knew that legally she must not open the drawers in the desk or the closet in the room.

"But maybe I can detect something without doing that," Nancy told herself.

The young sleuth circled the room, looking under the desk and a table, then on the shelves hugging one side of the room. By standing on tiptoe, she could just see what was inside several open boxes on the top shelf.

Suddenly Nancy gasped. "Giant firecrackers!" Lying on the shelf next to the telltale box were several sheets of the fire-dragon stationery!

"Oh, this is wonderful evidence!" the girl detective said to herself. "I think I had better report this to Captain Gray at once!"

As she turned to leave the room, Nancy became aware of a familiar voice in the shop. The speaker was Mrs. Horace Truesdale, the woman who had been in the store the first time Nancy had come there.

"Oh, dear!" Nancy said to herself. "Now I won't dare go out there. Mrs. Truesdale will be sure to see me and she's such a talker she'll certainly ask questions, and she may even tell Mr. Stromberg where I've been!"

The young sleuth decided there was nothing to do but wait for the woman to leave. But when she looked at her watch, she realized Mr. Stromberg might return at any minute.

Suddenly Nancy became aware of a scraping sound near her. Turning, she was just in time to see a trap door in the floor starting to lift.

"There's only one thing for me to do," Nancy thought wildly. "Hide! But where?"

CHAPTER XI

A Suspect Escapes

THERE was only one possible hiding place for Nancy Drew in the cluttered back office of the bookshop—under the kneehole desk. It had a solid front, but fortunately for Nancy it had a six-inch opening at the bottom.

Quickly the young sleuth crawled out of sight. By resting her cheek on the floor and peering out through the opening below the back panel, she could plainly see what was going on.

A moment later a man, carrying a large paper bag, stepped into the room. He was the driver who had trailed George to the hospital when she was masquerading as Chi Che! He was slender and rather short, but muscular looking. Could he be the man who had attacked Grandpa Soong, and the thief who had stolen the archaeologist's manuscript?

Nancy was greatly excited. There was no question now but that the Stromberg Bookshop *was* involved in the fire-dragon mystery!

"I wonder what this man is going to do?" the young sleuth asked herself.

Quietly he moved across the room, then he crouched and moved a carton away from one part of the wall. A small safe was revealed.

With deft fingers the man swung the dial left, right, left, then turned the handle. The door opened without a sound.

As the intruder scooped up a stack of papers tied with a cord, Nancy caught a quick glance at the top sheet. It was in Chinese writing.

"That may be Grandpa Soong's manuscript!" she told herself. "Do I dare try getting it away from him?"

Just then she heard Mr. Stromberg's voice in the bookshop. The intruder jammed the stack of papers into the bag he was carrying, and went to the trap door. Silently he descended and closed it behind him.

Nancy was thinking fast. She decided to avoid Mr. Stromberg if possible and follow the man with the manuscript. "And I'll notify the police about both of them," she told herself.

Nancy wriggled from under the desk, then tip-toed across the room and cautiously raised the trap door. Lying flat on the floor, she gazed into the cellar below. A bright light in the ceiling gave her a clear view of the place. No one was in sight.

"That man must have gone out the cellar door to the street," the young sleuth concluded. "Well, I'll do the same thing!"

Quickly she let herself down onto the narrow stairs and closed the trap door after her. Nancy descended and made her way to the front of the cellar. As she came out on the sidewalk Nancy felt sure that the manuscript thief could not be far away. She looked up, then down the street just in time to see the slender man disappear around the corner. She started running after him.

"Nancy!" cried a voice behind her, and a second later Bess and George caught up to her. "You had us scared silly!" Bess scolded. "What's going on?"

Nancy stopped short. Over her friend's shoulder she caught sight of Mr. Stromberg who was standing in the door of his shop looking at her angrily. Bess and George had revealed her getaway!

At once Nancy decided to give up the chase. "I can't explain now," she said. "Bess, go across the street to that drugstore and telephone Captain Gray. Tell him I have pretty good evidence that Mr. Stromberg is involved in some racket and ask him to send detectives here at once. Meanwhile, George and I will guard the store and cellar exits, so Mr. Stromberg can't get away."

By this time the shop owner had gone back inside. Bess hurried off to do the errand, as George and Nancy took up their posts. But Mr. Stromberg did not reappear. Within ten minutes two officers, Willet and Fisher, arrived. Nancy quickly explained the situation.

"We'll go in and talk to Mr. Stromberg," Officer Willet said. They entered, but were back in two minutes. "Mr. Stromberg isn't there," he reported.

Nancy frowned. "Did you look in the cellar? He may be hiding."

"Yes, we looked down there. Nobody around except that clerk in the shop. She's scared out of her wits and says she doesn't know where Mr. Stromberg went."

"There's only one answer," said Nancy. "There must be a secret exit."

While Officer Fisher remained to guard the street doors of the bookshop, Officer Willet accompanied the three girls into the shop. They went at once to the back room.

"There's a wall safe behind that carton," said Nancy. "Maybe there's another opening behind something else."

Against the far wall stood a very tall packing case. Nancy dashed over and peered behind it. "Here's the answer," she said. "There's a door leading outside. Mr. Stromberg must have escaped this way."

The officer and the girls squeezed behind the packing case and opened the door. They found themselves in the rear yard of a department store. They ran across it and went into the service entrance. No one was around.

"Luck was with Mr. Stromberg," Officer Willet said grimly.

The service entrance opened into the shipping room piled high with packages awaiting delivery. No shipping clerks seemed to be on duty. The officer and the girls rushed ahead until they came to swinging doors which opened into the first floor of the department store.

"Mr. Stromberg made an easy getaway," Willet remarked. "We may as well give up the chase and find him by some other method."

"You mean at his home?" George asked.

The officer nodded. He and the girls walked around the block until they came to the front of the bookshop. Officer Fisher was amazed to see the four arrive from this new direction. They quickly explained what had happened, then he reported that no one had come out of either entrance to the bookstore.

"Let's go back and see the clerk," Nancy proposed.

They entered the shop once more and Officer Willet asked the girl clerk where Mr. Stromberg lived.

"I—I d-don't k-know," the girl stammered. "I don't want to stay here. I don't like it. Please let me go home!"

"Not yet," the officer told her. "But don't be frightened. We'll take care of you. We just want you to tell us everything you know about Mr. Stromberg."

"N-nothing," the girl replied. "I was sent here by an employment agency that has my name. He called up for a clerk. He said another girl had worked here only a few hours."

"That's true," Nancy said.

Officer Willet looked through the desk for a clue to where Mr. Stromberg lived, but found nothing. He picked up a book of customers' names and read them carefully.

"I'll phone some of these people to see if they know where Mr. Stromberg lives," he said.

"I'd suggest that you try Mrs. Horace Truesdale first. She was in here two different times when I was, and seemed to know him well."

This attempt to locate the bookshop owner failed completely. Mrs. Truesdale said she had no idea where he lived. Other customers gave the same answer.

"I'll try some of the neighboring stores," the officer said, and went out. But he came back in a short time and reported that Mr. Stromberg, who had rented the shop six months before, was known as a very uncommunicative person and no one in the other shops knew where he lived.

"We're stymied for the time being," George admitted. "But we'll get those crooks yet!"

Officer Willet smiled. "I like your enthusiasm. I hope we can live up to your hopes."

Before leaving the shop, Nancy telephoned Captain Gray to tell him the unfortunate result of her endeavors to apprehend the suspects. He sympathized with her, then remarked philosophically:

"That's a detective's life! But we never give up."

He now reported that the police still had no clue to Chi Che Soong's whereabouts. Furthermore, according to the detective guarding the entrance to Aunt Eloise's apartment house, no suspicious person had been seen there.

"But something is bound to break soon," Captain Gray said. "We have so many police working on the case they're sure to find at least one of the suspects."

As the three girls started for Aunt Eloise Drew's apartment, all admitted to being a bit downcast. They had failed to learn anything more to help solve the mystery of Chi Che Soong's disappearance.

"Nancy," George said, "if that *was* the manuscript you saw being taken from the safe, why is Chi Che still being kept away from home?"

"I'm afraid," Nancy replied, "there's another reason for her disappearance besides someone wanting to get hold of Grandpa Soong's work. I believe Chi Che inadvertently found out about some kind of racket, and the gang involved is giving her no chance to report it to the police."

Bess sighed. "Oh, dear! The poor girl!"

That evening Nancy received a telephone call from Lily Alys Wu. The Chinese girl asked what progress had been made on the case. Upon hearing the latest developments, she expressed her own great concern about Chi Che.

"What's worse," she added, "I've seen Mr. Soong, and I'm afraid he senses now that something is wrong. He doesn't seem too well and he isn't doing any writing."

"How dreadful!" Nancy exclaimed. "I'll run up to the hospital as soon as I can and try to cheer him a bit."

"What do you think Mr. Stromberg is going to do now?" Lily Alys asked.

Nancy thought a few seconds, then replied, "I'm afraid he and his pals may skip the country. It's my guess they may even go to Hong Kong."

Suddenly Lily Alys broke in excitedly, "Nancy, I just thought of something that may help you solve the mystery!"

CHAPTER XII

Flight Plans

"WHILE I was working in the bookshop," Lily Alys told Nancy, "I walked to the back room to ask Mr. Stromberg a question. Just like the other time I told you about, he was talking on the phone in a low tone.

"But I caught one thing he said that might have something to do with your case. He said to the other person, 'You have your ticket? No one will —— with all those students.' I didn't catch the one part of the sentence." Lily Alys asked Nancy what she thought the missing word might be.

"It could be any number of things," Nancy said slowly. "Of course it might be something completely innocent. But if Mr. Stromberg were talking to one of the gang, the missing part might have been 'recognize you' or 'suspect you.'"

"It probably was," the Chinese girl agreed. "I wonder who the person could have been?"

"And I wonder," said Nancy, "what the ticket is for. It might be for travel, for the theater, for some sports event—"

"That is one reason I called you," Lily Alys broke in quickly. "I said maybe I could help you. On a certain flight to Hong Kong from New York, the whole tourist section of the plane has been reserved for Chinese and American students from Columbia University."

Nancy was excited over the information. "Only I doubt that any students are mixed up in this racket of Mr. Stromberg's."

Lily Alys said she was not thinking of the tourist section of the plane. "The first-class section is open to all passengers. I thought the person Mr. Stromberg was talking to might possibly be among those people."

Nancy was thrilled. "Lily Alys, I believe this is a stroke of genius on your part. How soon does this plane leave?"

"In three days. It's for a ten-day vacation in Hong Kong." Lily Alys chuckled softly. "I understand that the tourist section has not been entirely filled. Perhaps, if you care to go to Hong Kong yourself, I can arrange for you to have one of the seats."

Nancy felt a surge of excitement over this possibility. She thanked Lily Alys and said she would let her know if she wanted a reservation. "As a matter of fact, my father and I were planning to go to Hong Kong sometime soon. Maybe we could take this flight!"

"But the tourist section is only for students," Lily Alys reminded the young sleuth.

"My father could go first class," Nancy told her. "He might spot the suspect without being recognized. I'll try to obtain a list of the passengers who have signed up so far."

"Do you think Mr. Stromberg may be one of them?" the Chinese girl asked.

"Possibly," Nancy replied. "But if so, I'm sure he'll be traveling under an assumed name and I would have to see him to identify him. But I can alert the police, anyway, and also tell them other members of the gang may be aboard."

She thanked Lily Alys for the helpful information, then at once called Captain Gray. He too felt that perhaps Nancy had picked up an important clue. "I'll call you back and read you the list of first-class passengers," he promised, "as soon as I get them."

Hardly half an hour had gone by when he telephoned. The passengers' names were in alphabetical order and none was familiar to Nancy until he came to the T's.

"Mrs. Horace Truesdale!" Nancy exclaimed.

"You know her?" the officer asked quickly.

"Well, no, not exactly. But twice I saw her in Stromberg's Bookshop. She seemed to be a regular customer."

"That doesn't prove anything, of course," Captain Gray said. "Nevertheless, I will find out more about her and let you know." He read the rest of the list of passengers but none was known to Nancy.

Within a short time the officer once more called Nancy, this time to report that there was nothing suspicious about Mrs. Horace Truesdale. She was a widow who lived alone in a middle-class apartment house. "She's reputed to be a great reader and often goes on trips to visit friends."

The officer finished his conversation by telling Nancy that there still was no news on any of the suspects in the Chi Che Soong case. "But members of the force will be on hand to watch everyone boarding the plane to Hong Kong."

Later that evening Nancy telephoned her father and asked him how soon he was going to Hong Kong. The lawyer chuckled. " 'Fess up, my dear. What's on your mind?"

His daughter laughed, then quickly related the entire story regarding recent developments in the mystery and told him of the flight to Hong Kong which some Columbia students were taking.

"I'd like to go on the flight," Nancy said. "And, Dad, I wish that you would go along in the first-class section. You could look over the passengers to see if you think any of them might be suspects."

After a pause, Mr. Drew said, "I believe I

could leave here in a couple of days. That would work out very nicely. I really should get to Hong Kong to interview the heirs involved in that contested will I told you about."

After further conversation, father and daughter agreed that it might be wise if the two traveled as if they were strangers.

"I'm sure," the lawyer added, "that the plan will work out to good advantage."

Nancy said she had another request to make. "I'd love to have Bess and George accompany us."

Mr. Drew approved this idea at once. "The girls will not only help you, but may prove to be a safety factor. I'll phone the Marvins and Faynes and find out if they'll give permission."

"Wonderful!" Nancy exclaimed. Then she giggled, saying as she had done ever since she was a little girl, "I'll keep my fingers crossed!"

"I suppose," said Mr. Drew, "that you will want to make your own reservations through Columbia University. I'll let you know the result of my calls to Bess's and George's families. Then you can borrow money from your Aunt Eloise to purchase the tickets."

"And I'll notify Ned Nickerson of our coming," Nancy added. "He can arrange accommodations for us in Hong Kong."

"A good idea," Mr. Drew approved. "But I think I had better do this, in case you're being watched. One of the gang might pick up the information."

"All right, Dad."

Within an hour Mr. Drew called back to say that Bess and George had been given permission to go on the trip.

Nancy's chums were elated. "Oh, boy!" George cried. "If Chi Che is in Hong Kong, what a ball we'll have while finding her!"

"Yes," said Bess. "But we just must save some time to buy clothes there." Then she twinkled. "Do you suppose Ned will bring along a couple of dates for George and me?"

George grinned. "He probably will. But maybe you'd better go on a diet, Bess. Your huge appetite may frighten the boys away."

The other girls laughed. "Oh, *George!*" What had started out to be a worrisome evening now took a turn of merriment. Nancy used the kitchen phone to call Lily Alys, and asked her to get plane reservations for the three girls in the tourist section of the Hong Kong flight.

"This is very exciting," said the Chinese girl. "I hope you have a wonderful time and solve the mystery also. I shall find out at once about getting seats on the plane and call you back."

For the second time that evening Nancy received good news. The three seats were available. Lily Alys told Nancy where at the university she could pay for the reservations.

"There is only one possible worry," the Chinese girl said. "If any Columbia students wish to make last-minute reservations, you will have to give up the seats."

"I understand," said Nancy. To herself, she added that she would cross her fingers!

Bess and George declared they too fervently hoped that their trip to Hong Kong would not have to be canceled. As the girls prepared for bed, they discussed the clothes they would need.

"I guess," Nancy decided, "the clothes we have with us will be plenty for the trip. We'll be buying more abroad, anyhow."

"Isn't it fortunate that we all had vaccinations recently?" Bess said happily.

"It certainly is," Nancy agreed. "And I've heard that it's possible to obtain passports right here in New York in case of emergency! I'm sure Captain Gray will certify to the emergency for us."

As Aunt Eloise and her three guests were preparing breakfast in the kitchen the next morning, Nancy said, "I'd like to go to Chinatown once more and see if I can pick up any further clues in the mystery."

"Suppose we go this evening and have dinner," Miss Drew suggested. "There is a delightful restaurant only two doors from that shop where you found the fire-dragon stationery, Nancy."

This plan was agreed upon. The group decided to arrive promptly at six o'clock, since Aunt Eloise said that all the food was cooked to order and there would be a long wait.

"I want to visit that stationery store again," Nancy said. "I know it's open in the evening. While we're waiting for dinner to be cooked, I can go there and talk to the proprietor. Maybe some of the gang have been in his shop again."

At exactly six o'clock Nancy and her friends entered the attractive restaurant. All the Chinese and American diners were eating their food with chopsticks.

"I'll never be able to manage that and get enough to eat!" Bess said. Her companions laughed.

Aunt Eloise and the girls ordered Peking duck and bean sprouts which were to follow birds'-nest soup.

"And now if you'll excuse me a few minutes," said Nancy, "I'll just walk over to the stationery store."

Nancy went out to the narrow sidewalk and turned toward the shop. As she passed the next store, with apartments above it, an object came hurtling down toward her.

The next second it hit Nancy squarely on the back of the head. She fell to the pavement, unconscious!

CHAPTER XIII

An Ominous Dream

As NANCY lay unconscious on the sidewalk, people began to run from all directions to assist her. The excitement was heard in the restaurant. Aunt Eloise, Bess, and George dashed outside.

"Oh, Nancy!" her aunt cried, hurrying to her side. "What happened?" she asked the bystanders.

A Chinese man pointed to a large, broken flowerpot on the pavement. "This apparently fell on the young lady. Can I be of help to you?"

"It is pretty chilly out here," Aunt Eloise said. "I think we should carry my niece into the restaurant."

By this time Nancy's eyelids were fluttering. Bess and George sighed in relief, sure she would be all right. George decided to stay outside as strong arms carried Nancy to the restaurant.

"Bess, I'm going to find out how this flowerpot

happened to fall," George declared, holding her cousin back. "Maybe it toppled off a window sill accidentally, but on the other hand it might have been thrown deliberately."

Bess nodded grimly. She looked upward above the store front and said, "There's a light in the second-floor apartment, but not in the third."

"I think we should investigate both places." George spoke with determination.

She picked up a piece of newspaper which had been dropped on the sidewalk and scooped up the plant and the earth. The two girls opened a door to the apartment stairway and ascended. They rang the bell to the second-floor flat. It was opened by a Chinese woman who looked at Bess and George curiously.

"Yes, please?" she asked.

"Does this plant belong to you?" George asked. "It fell from up here, somewhere."

"No, it is not mine," the woman answered.

"Do you know where it came from?" Bess queried.

"I cannot say," the Chinese answered. "But my neighbor upstairs has one like it."

"Then perhaps it fell from her window," George suggested.

"No, oh no," the woman said. "Mrs. Lin Tang is not at home. She has gone away to visit relatives."

George asked if anyone else lived in the apartment upstairs who might be at home. The woman shook her head. Then, looking intently at the girls, she said, "I *did* hear someone coming down the stairs. But when I heard the excitement on the street, I ran to look out and forgot about the footsteps until now."

"Did you see anyone leave this building?" George queried.

"No, I am sorry. I did not."

"Let's go upstairs and see if one of your neighbor's plants is missing," Bess proposed to the woman.

The three hurried up the stairway to the third floor, but the door to the apartment there was closed and locked.

"The intruder must have had a skeleton key and let himself in," George remarked. "Let's go back to the street and find out if anyone saw a person coming from the front entrance."

The Chinese woman said she would take the plant and repot it. The two girls thanked her and hurried down to the sidewalk. They began asking the people still standing around if they had noticed anyone leaving the apartment, but all said no.

Bess and George then returned to the restaurant and were delighted to see that Nancy was fully conscious. She was lying on a couch in the private office of the owner. The room contained many lovely Chinese decorations.

"Hi, girls!" she said, but the cousins noticed that she was very pale and her voice sounded weak.

"I'm so thankful the accident was no worse," Aunt Eloise said. "But we're going home. Mr. Wong, the owner, has kindly consented to pack our dinner to take with us. We'll eat it in the apartment. Nancy should go right to bed."

At that moment the outer door of the restaurant suddenly burst open and a group came directly into the office. A red-haired man was being hauled in by a policeman and two Chinese men. Nancy sat up.

The officer began to speak. "These two men"—

he indicated the Chinese—"say this man ran from the building after the accident. They had seen the flowerpot hurtle down and thought he might have tossed it on purpose, so they went after him. I was on the corner and took up the chase. Have any of you ever seen him before?"

"I'll say I have!" George declared. "He tried to kidnap me once!"

"And me another time!" Bess added.

"What!" the policeman exclaimed.

"You're crazy!" the prisoner shouted. "I never saw these girls before in my life!"

"Perhaps you don't recognize me," George said

with a bitter smile. "The last time you saw me, you thought I was Chi Che Soong."

The man started perceptibly, but he kept up his bluster. "Officer, this is ridiculous. I admit I was in the apartment house. I went to the third floor to visit the people there but nobody was at home. I don't know anything about a flowerpot. You have no right to hold me."

"Yes he has," Bess spoke up. "My friend Nancy Drew and I were trailing you that day you tried to kidnap my cousin. You found out from the driver of the stolen car that you had grabbed the wrong girl. Then you jumped into the car alone and raced off with the driver. We found out later you had stolen the car."

"There's not a word of truth in what she's saying," the prisoner insisted. "I'm leaving!"

"You'd better not even try," the policeman told him firmly. "Is there anything else you girls can tell me about this man?"

Nancy answered. "Everything my friends have said really happened, Officer. Also, the driver who was waiting for this man told him he had phoned to somebody named Ryle." She turned to the prisoner. "Who is he?"

"I don't know anybody by that name," the man replied defiantly.

"Suppose you tell us who *you* are," the policeman prompted.

The man refused to talk, so the officer went

through his pockets. He pulled out a wallet and opened it. It contained a driver's license issued to Ferdinand Breen.

"I think we have enough evidence to hold you, Breen," the officer stated.

"If you don't," George spoke up, "here is something else. We heard that the man named Ryle and a companion were trying to sell some jade that was thought to have been smuggled into this country."

Once more the prisoner jumped and gave George an angry look. But he said nothing.

The policeman asked to use the desk telephone. Mr. Wong nodded and the officer called for a patrol car. Soon it arrived and the prisoner was led away.

"I'm sorry that you have had this unpleasant interruption in your business," Aunt Eloise apologized to Mr. Wong.

"I am always glad to see law and order carried out." The restaurant owner bowed. "Please, Miss Drew, do not let the matter disturb you. The package containing your dinner is ready. I have called a taxi and it is waiting at the door."

"Thank you very much," Aunt Eloise and the girls said, as Nancy arose and they walked out. Nancy added, "I spoiled our little party, but someday I shall come back."

Mr. Wong smiled and said he was glad to hear this. As soon as they reached Aunt Eloise's apart-

ment, Nancy had some hot tea and went to bed.
Soon she was sound asleep. After the others had
eaten the delicious Chinese food, George said, "It
isn't too late. Bess, let's go to the hospital and see
Grandpa Soong. Maybe we can cheer him up."

"You're not going to tell him what happened today?" Miss Drew asked quickly.

"Oh, no," George replied.

"All right," Aunt Eloise said. "But please take a
taxi both ways for safety."

The two girls promised to do so and left. Aunt
Eloise went to the telephone and called Captain
Gray to relay the Chinatown incident. He told
her he had just read of Breen's arrest on the police
teletype. The officer inquired solicitously about
Nancy's health and was relieved to hear she had
not been severely injured. "I am going to talk to
the prisoner right now," he said.

Bess and George reached the hospital only
twenty minutes before visiting hours would be
over.

The cousins were shocked when they saw
Grandpa Soong. He was very listless and pale. A
nurse who was in the room told them he had
eaten practically nothing that day.

"I am not hungry," the Chinese said weakly.
"I am greatly worried about my Chi Che."

The nurse stepped from the room and both
George and Bess tried to bolster the man's lagging

spirits by remarking that Chi Che probably was having a delightful time with her friends. To their amazement the elderly man shook his head.

"At first I believed that what Chi Che wrote was true," he said. "But now I am sure something has happened to her. We must have enemies— I do not know why. For a while I thought Chi Che was being held until the thief who took my manuscript could accomplish that evil deed. Then she would return. But she has not come back."

Bess and George looked at each other, at a loss for words. Grandpa Soong went on, "I had a strange dream. Chi Che was far away. She was being guarded by a fire dragon and was unable to escape. My poor Chi Che! She kept calling to me and to Miss Eloise Drew to save her."

Bess leaned forward and took the elderly man's hand in her own. "Grandpa Soong," she said, "that was a frightening dream. But you know that really there are no dragons."

The patient had been staring into space as if in a trance. Bess was sure he had not heard a word she said. Presently he asked:

"Do you girls believe in thought transference?"

They both admitted that they did. Then Grandpa Soong said, "There are men in this world who are more dangerous than fire dragons. I am sure my Chi Che is being held by one or more of them and really was calling out in her thoughts to me and to Miss Drew for help."

George felt that since Grandpa Soong was so suspicious of the truth, Nancy would agree that this was an appropriate time to reveal some of the girls' findings in connection with his granddaughter's absence. She told him about the various episodes in the bookshop where Chi Che had worked, including the fact that Nancy had seen a man open the safe in the private office and take out what appeared to be a manuscript.

"We all think it was your stolen work," George went on.

"The police have been notified?" Grandpa Soong asked excitedly.

"Yes," George replied. "One of those 'dragons' is now in jail."

"Did he reveal where my Chi Che is?" the elderly man queried.

"Unfortunately, no," George answered. "But we have several clues to the rest of the gang."

George stopped speaking, for at this moment the nurse returned. She had a delicious-looking eggnog on a tray.

"Mr. Soong, won't you please drink this?" she asked, smiling.

Without being helped, the elderly man suddenly sat up in bed. "I feel much better," he said. "My visitors have cheered me considerably. Yes, I will drink the eggnog."

The nurse looked pleased. She set it on his night stand and again went off. As Grandpa

Soong sipped the drink, he begged to hear more.

Bess and George told how Mr. Stromberg seemed to be mixed up with the "dragons" and that it was just possible he and some of his friends had fled to Hong Kong.

"Nancy and George and I are flying to Hong Kong in a couple of days," Bess told him.

"Hong Kong!" Grandpa Soong repeated excitedly. "If my Chi Che has been taken there, she surely will be found. That is my twin brother's home. You must contact him as soon as you arrive."

"We will be very glad to do that," Bess said.

"My brother, Lee Soong, is retired now," Grandpa Soong went on. "But at one time he was head of the police department of Shanghai."

"Oh, this is wonderful news!" Bess exclaimed. "We will all work together. Between the New York and Hong Kong police and your brother and Nancy Drew, this mystery should be solved very quickly!"

A bell rang, indicating visiting hours were over. The girls quickly said good-by to Mr. Soong. They could hardly wait to get home and tell their news about the Shanghai ex-police chief Mr. Lee Soong.

Aunt Eloise opened the apartment door. "Sh!" she said. "Nancy mustn't hear me, but I'm terribly worried!"

CHAPTER XIV

A Hidden Microphone

"Nancy is worse?" Bess and George cried together fearfully.

"No," Aunt Eloise replied. "Come in and I'll tell you."

When the three were huddled in the living room, the older woman whispered, "A little while ago I had a threatening phone call. The man said 'This snooping into other people's affairs by Nancy Drew has got to stop! And if she goes on that plane, it'll be blown up!'"

"Oh, how horrible!" Bess exclaimed in an undertone.

George, equally worried, frowned. She rarely paid attention to anonymous threats, but for Nancy's sake she felt this one could not be overlooked. "That man probably means what he says!"

"It is a dreadful situation," Aunt Eloise remarked. "Perhaps, in order to save many lives, you girls should give up the trip."

Bess was inclined to agree but George declared she was not going to let any dragon scare her off. "Anyhow, let's wait until morning and see what Nancy thinks."

The three went to bed but slept fitfully. They were concerned about the dangers which they had experienced in connection with the case.

The following morning Nancy was up, and except for a sore bruise on the back of her head, she declared she was back to normal. As the group cooked breakfast, they discussed the happenings of the evening before at great length—Nancy's accident, Grandpa Soong's story of his brother, and finally the threatening telephone message.

"The gang certainly has a good spy system," Nancy remarked, puzzled. "How in the world do they find out all our plans?"

Then suddenly she put her forefinger to her lips. The others kept quiet as she began to tiptoe around, looking behind the stove, the refrigerator, inside the cabinets, and finally back of the dainty curtains at the windows.

Presently Nancy nodded and motioned the others to come forward. She pointed out a tiny disk fastened to the window frame under the valance of the curtain. From the disk a tiny wire ran outside the window and down the side of the building.

Nancy picked up an order pad and pencil. On it she wrote:

"That disk is a microphone, and probably was hidden here the day the intruder broke in. Our enemies have been picking up all our conversations in the kitchen and recording them somewhere below. I suggest that we turn the tables. Let's all talk as if we were worried to death about the bomb scare and are going to give up the plane trip."

The others, astonished, nodded. Then Aunt Eloise began the conversation.

"Why are you girls so quiet?" she asked. "Don't tell me. I know. You're all very brave but this bomb threat really has you upset."

"I'm afraid you're right," said Bess, making her voice tremble. "I don't know about the rest of you but I'd like to be counted out. I'm sure my mother and dad would never approve of my going on a plane that might be blown up!"

"You have a point there," George agreed. "If my parents knew about this, they'd put both feet down hard. But it burns me up. Here I was looking forward to a nice trip and someone we don't know steps in and ruins everything."

"Yes," said Nancy. She gave a tremendous sigh. "We were just getting some good clues and now this has to happen. Well, I suppose I'd better call my dad and tell him we're canceling our flight tomorrow. He'll be angry, I know, but I'm sure he'll tell me to stay home."

"Do you think we could keep on with our

sleuthing in New York City?" George put in.

Nancy said she wondered whether this would be worth while. She was sure that most of the members of the gang who were holding Chi Che had left town. "Otherwise," she added, "the police would have picked them up."

Aunt Eloise Drew remarked that she was so sorry everything had turned out the way it had. She laughed. "I suppose, Nancy, you can't expect good luck in solving every mystery you undertake."

"No," her niece agreed. "Just the same, I hate to leave Chi Che in such a dangerous situation."

"Yes," said Bess, giving a little sob. "Goodness only knows what torture they may be putting her through."

"Then we're all agreed we're giving up the trip?" Nancy asked. There was a chorus of "ayes."

The group stopped speaking. Nancy opened a cabinet drawer and took out a pair of scissors with wooden handles. Then, closing the window tight on the wire, she snipped it and wound the outer end around the curtain rod to keep it from falling to the ground when the window was opened again.

As George started to speak, the young sleuth held her finger to her lips. Once more signaling to the others to follow, she began a systematic search of the rest of the apartment to locate any other hidden microphones. But a thorough hunt revealed that the only one seemed to be in the kitchen.

Bess flopped into a chair. "Nancy Drew, you're something!"

"You sure are," George agreed. "I almost talked myself into giving up that trip during our act, but I'm not going to!"

"Nor I!" said Nancy.

Bess was a little more hesitant but finally decided that their broadcast had been convincing enough to keep any of the gang from placing a bomb on the plane.

Nancy now went to the telephone and called Captain Gray. When she had explained the whole incident, he said he would detail two men to shadow the person who came to pick up the record.

"No doubt it's in some device hidden at the ground level of the apartment house," the officer surmised. "We'll let the fellow hang himself so to speak. That is, we'll give him a chance to pass the word along that you girls have given up your sleuthing, then we'll nab him. I'll keep you posted."

After breakfast Aunt Eloise went off to school. The three girls met Captain Gray at the passport office, where he vouched for the emergency aspect of their flight. Passports were quickly issued.

"I'll call you as soon as we have any news on the tape recorder," the officer said as he dropped the girls at Aunt Eloise's apartment.

Later that afternoon when the telephone rang, Nancy ran to answer it. Captain Gray was on the line. "Good news, Nancy," he said. "We picked up the man responsible for the hidden mike and tape recorder at the apartment house. We gave him time to listen to what all of you had said and go to a phone booth.

"One of our plain-clothes men was nearby. He knew from the spaces between the numbers and letters what the fellow was dialing. Then our men picked him up. In the meantime, we were able to locate the party he called—a man known as Smitty. We find he was the one who accompanied Breen to Chinatown the day you chased them."

Nancy was thrilled to hear this. "And who was the man you picked up in the phone booth?"

Captain Gray chuckled. "One of the top members of the gang. His name is Reilley Moot. His nickname is Ryle."

"Oh, that's marvelous!" Nancy exclaimed. "And has he confessed to anything?"

"Not exactly," the officer answered. "But we found a giant firecracker in his pocket."

"*He* must be the one responsible for causing the explosions here!" Nancy broke in.

"Right. Looks as if things are closing in on

the gang," the captain said. "You've done some fine sleuthing, Nancy. The police department can never thank you adequately."

He added that through communications received from Interpol, the police thought the men who were in jail, and their accomplices still at large, were members of a large smuggling ring.

"Just what they're smuggling we don't know," the officer went on. "But we hope to find out soon." He laughed. "If their headquarters are in Hong Kong, perhaps you will find out what they're smuggling before we do!"

"That sounds almost like an assignment." Nancy laughed too. Then she became serious. "Captain Gray, there is one thing which is being overlooked and to me that is the most important of all—finding Chi Che Soong."

She begged the officer to concentrate on that angle of the mystery, then said good-by. Before long, Aunt Eloise came home and announced she was going to take the girls to the theater. "I suggest that we do not mention the mystery or your future plans just in case any spies may be following us," she advised.

The girls agreed and dressed for the festive evening. They had dinner at an uptown French restaurant, then saw a gay musical comedy.

"New York is just thrilling!" Bess exclaimed as they emerged from the theater.

Nancy and George echoed this and Nancy

added, "Thanks a million, Aunt Eloise. This has been a terrific farewell party."

The following morning Miss Drew and the girls exchanged fond good-bys. Aunt Eloise said it had been a wonderful visit and she hoped they would soon come again.

At three o'clock the girls set off. To keep any spies from suspecting they were headed for the International Airport, Nancy asked their taxi driver to take them to Grand Central Station. Once there, she had him drive on and finally head for the East Side Airlines Terminal. There the girls' baggage was weighed and the travelers hurried into a limousine which took them to the airport.

Almost the first person Nancy saw in the waiting room was her father. But as previously arranged, Mr. Drew and his daughter pretended not to recognize each other.

The three girls stood a little distance from the ramp and closely watched each passenger go aboard their plane. The only one they recognized was Mrs. Horace Truesdale. Finally Nancy and her companions were warned by a loudspeaker announcement to go aboard.

Quickly they got on the plane and showed their tickets to the stewardess. To the girls' annoyance, Mrs. Truesdale was standing just beyond the doorway. She looked at them in amazement.

"Why, when did you decide to come on this

trip?" she asked. "Are you students at the university? Or are you traveling first class?"

"Neither," Nancy replied, and started toward the rear of the plane.

"Are you going to Hong Kong?" Mrs. Truesdale persisted.

"Isn't everyone on board?" Nancy countered.

"Will you be visiting friends over there?" the woman pursued.

"Yes," Nancy replied. Secretly she was thinking that this overly inquisitive woman might try to be friendly with the girls in Hong Kong and interfere with their sleuthing.

The stewardess asked Mrs. Truesdale please to take her seat and motioned for the girls to go to theirs. Finally the lights went on, requesting passengers to fasten their seat belts. The door was closed and locked. The giant engines roared, and finally the plane taxied to the end of the runway.

After the great craft had stood there for over ten minutes, Bess said to Nancy and George seated alongside her, "Why don't we take off?"

At that moment the stewardess's voice came over the loud-speaker. "Your attention, please! On order of the police department all hand luggage must be examined. Will you please co-operate?"

Nancy, Bess, and George looked at one another. Were the police, perhaps, looking for a bomb after all?

CHAPTER XV

The Mah-jongg Dealer

"LET's get off the plane!" Bess urged in a tense whisper.

Nancy shook her head. "Maybe it isn't a bomb. Perhaps someone is trying to smuggle goods out of the United States."

The student group sat in strained silence. They could plainly hear a woman in the first-class section arguing loudly. Nancy recognized Mrs. Truesdale's voice.

"This is an outrage!" she was shouting. "I am telling you here and now that it's a disgraceful procedure. Can't a person take a trip out of the United States without being treated like a common thief?"

Nancy and her friends had to smile in spite of the fact that there might be a bomb aboard. George remarked, "That woman is a pain!"

Presently two police officers came to the rear part of the aircraft and inspected everyone's hand luggage. As they finished their checkup, and started toward the door, Nancy asked them, "Could you tell us why you searched our bags, or is that against regulations?"

One of the officers looked at her intently, then said, "I'm sure there's no harm in telling you. Someone phoned the airport that a bomb was being carried in the hand luggage of a passenger on this plane. It must have been a crank. We did not find anything."

"Thank goodness," said Bess.

The officers left the plane, and a few minutes later the craft finally took off. It had been in the air about an hour when Nancy saw her father walking back toward her.

"I think it's all right now for me to speak to you," he said, a twinkle in his eye.

The lawyer perched on the arm of his daughter's chair. "I've been engaging various men in conversation," he said in a low tone. "All seem to be in legitimate businesses. I'm sure there are no suspects among them."

"Did you know that the police were looking for a bomb?" Nancy asked.

Mr. Drew nodded.

Nancy told him about the bomb threat the girls had received and about her own ruse to keep one from being placed in the plane.

Mr. Drew frowned. "I believe your trick worked for a while, but the gang probably had you trailed to be sure. There was no time to place a bomb aboard, but they still hoped to scare you and try to keep you from going to Hong Kong."

Nancy whispered, "This must surely mean the gang has transferred its operations to Hong Kong."

Mr. Drew agreed. He got up and returned to his seat.

Gradually, during the flight, Nancy made the acquaintance of the students, and in her own subtle way quizzed each one to see if by any chance there was a suspect among them. She came to the conclusion there was none.

"Members of the gang holding Chi Che must have gone by some other route," the girl detective told herself.

The great plane stopped at Anchorage, Alaska, for refueling. Nancy and her friends were intrigued by the beautiful city. They were amazed at its size and the tall modern buildings.

"This used to be the capital," said Bess, "but now Juneau is."

Nancy remarked, "I'd love to come to Alaska in the middle of winter, and ride on a dog sled!"

The travelers' next landing was Tokyo, Japan. What a bustling place the airport was! The girls were fascinated by the native people, most of whom wore Western dress, but many had on kimonos and sandals. Everyone seemed good-natured and there was lots of laughter. Men and women always bowed low to one another in greeting or when saying good-by.

The twenty minutes during which the travelers were allowed to visit the terminal were soon up, and Nancy and her friends climbed back into the plane. It was now two o'clock Sunday afternoon. By the time they reached their destination, it was exactly eleven hours later than it was in New York.

As the plane began its Hong Kong descent, George looked at her watch and grinned. "It's one o'clock yesterday afternoon in New York," she said.

The plane set down and taxied toward the airport building. The landing and take-off strips of Kai Tak Airport fascinated Nancy. They were on a spit of man-made land and she realized how skillful a pilot had to be to use them.

"We're on the China mainland," said Bess. "Not Hong Kong Island at all."

"That's right," said George, who had studied the map. "This Kai Tak Airport actually is in the city of Kowloon."

"How do you get over to Hong Kong Island?" Bess queried.

"By ferry," George replied.

All this time Nancy, who now had a window seat, was looking intently at the crowd of people waiting behind a wire-mesh fence. She hoped to see Ned Nickerson among them!

"Oh, there he is!" A tingle of excitement rushed up and down Nancy's spine.

The plane stopped and the exit door was opened. First-class passengers disembarked. Mr. Drew hurried toward the fence behind which he had spied Ned Nickerson.

"Hello, Mr. Drew!" the tall, good-looking, athletic young man called. "Where are the girls?"

"They're coming." The lawyer laughed. "I traveled in style. They're in the tourist section."

At that very moment the girls were moving toward the exit. George was saying, "I hope that pesky Mrs. Truesdale won't stop us and try to find out what we're going to do."

The three girls finally went down the steps and exchanged gay greetings with Ned through the wire fence. Then the four travelers entered the low, white administration building. Here they went through the immigration formalities and customs examination. Finally they collected their baggage, then hurried to meet Ned in the waiting room.

"It's sure good to see you," the young man said, giving Mr. Drew a hearty handshake and kissing each of the girls. "I have a jalopy outside. I guess we can all crowd into it."

"Did you get us hotel accommodations?" Mr. Drew asked him.

"Yes, at the Peninsula Hotel. That's right here in Kowloon and I'm sure you will like it." He chuckled. "Since prices here are lower than in the States, I engaged a three-bedroom suite with a living room. Nancy may want to entertain one or more villains."

"Including yourself?" Nancy teased.

"Call me anything you like," Ned responded, "but just let me stick around."

"How much time can you spend away from Chung Chi College?" Nancy asked him.

"A few days. Well, shall we go?"

Ned escorted the group outside the building. Two porters stowed the luggage in Ned's small foreign car, then everyone got in. Bess giggled. "It's a tight squeeze!"

As the visitors approached the business section of Kowloon, they became more and more intrigued with the city. Most of the buildings were not more than three stories high, and Chinese signs hung everywhere. There were many Western people walking about, but the bulk of the populace was Chinese. Native men, women, and children wore pants and loose-fitting straight jackets. Most of the suits were black and plain, but here and there one would see someone wearing a beautifully embroidered garment.

Presently Ned drove to the hotel and residential area, where the streets were broad. The Peninsula Hotel was a large, attractive building. They entered the long, curving driveway and alighted at the front entrance.

"This is very charming," Mr. Drew remarked as the travelers walked through the lobby to the registration desk.

The whole central section was filled with couches, lounge chairs, palms, flowers, and tea tables. People, seated in groups, were sipping tea and eating small cakes.

As soon as the Drews and their friends had unpacked and freshened up a bit, they met in their living room. Ned demanded to hear all about the mystery on which the three girls had been working. When they finished telling him, he whistled and said:

"You really picked a honey this time, Nancy. So you think Chi Che might be a prisoner here in Hong Kong?"

"I believe there's a good possibility. But even if she isn't, I'm sure this is headquarters for the smuggling ring, and that she knows their secret. If the leaders can be rounded up, Chi Che will automatically be released."

"I'm ready to help," Ned said. "Nancy, when, where, and how do I start?"

The young sleuth thought for a moment, then she replied, "I want to show you something in my handbag."

Nancy obtained the bag from her bedroom and took out the two pages which she had torn from the book on Asia. "These are the sheets which upset Mr. Stromberg. Lily Alys said the words 'mah-jongg sets' had been underlined. I don't believe she noticed in which shop. Now's your chance to be a detective, Ned."

The young man took the sheets and read them carefully. Then a smile spread over his face. "I think I have a clue for you, Nancy," he said. "One of these shops is owned by a man named Lung. The word *lung* was the original Chinese name for dragon."

"Of course!" Nancy said excitedly. "I remember now! Grandpa Soong told us that. Let's go there first thing tomorrow morning."

"Fine," Ned agreed.

"George," said Bess, "this is our chance to go shopping for clothes and souvenirs."

The next morning Nancy and Ned started out directly after breakfast. They took Ned's car to the ferry, parked it, and went by boat to Hong Kong Island. As they crossed the bay, Nancy marveled at the surrounding scenery. The harbor was filled with boats of all kinds, large and small, including junks and sampans. The island ahead of them was almost like a stone fortress which rose to a pinnacle in the center.

"That is Victoria Peak and it's eighteen hundred and nine feet high," Ned told Nancy.

"It's amazing how they build houses right into the side of the mountain," Nancy remarked.

When she and Ned debarked, he hailed two

rickshas and the couple climbed into them. Nancy was intrigued by the man pulling her little two-wheeled vehicle. He trotted along after Ned's ricksha at a pace that a horse would trot.

Nancy found Hong Kong a fascinating combination of modern skyscrapers and quaint Oriental buildings. Presently the ricksha men turned down an alley and in a few minutes stopped. They had arrived at Mr. Lung's shop.

"Like the ride?" Ned grinned.

"It was fun," Nancy replied as they alighted.

She and Ned entered the shop and gazed around at the wall decorations. Every one of them was a dragon in some form. There were painted scrolls, pictures, and a few wooden figures. Nancy shivered. "This is a creepy place," she whispered.

There was a short counter toward the rear of the shallow shop. As the couple approached it, a man came from behind a curtain in back of the counter.

"Mr. Lung?" Ned asked.

The man nodded.

"We'd like to see some mah-jongg sets," Ned told him.

Without a word the shop owner took several from a shelf and gave the price of each. All the playing pieces were of ivory, but the less expensive sets were in plain boxes, while others were in carved teakwood chests lined with camphor wood.

"These are very beautiful," Nancy said. "Do you have any others?"

Mr. Lung shook his head. "We have more that are similar, but these are samples of all the varieties I carry."

Nancy examined the boxes carefully. It occurred to her that each one contained many places in which small articles could be secreted for smuggling.

"What do you think?" Ned asked her, careful not to use Nancy's name.

"Let's decide later," the young sleuth answered. "After all, we've just started to shop." She turned to Mr. Lung. "Thank you very much. We'll probably be back."

The man bowed and started to put the mah-jongg sets back on the shelf. Nancy and Ned left the shop and strolled up the alleyway. They had not gone far when Nancy heard a woman's familiar voice say loudly, "You charge too much!"

Turning, the girl saw Mrs. Horace Truesdale just alighting from a ricksha. The woman, frowning, put some money in the man's hand, then walked into Mr. Lung's shop.

Quickly Nancy told Ned of her encounter with Mrs. Truesdale, then whispered tensely:

"Is it just a coincidence that she knows Mr. Stromberg and came directly here to Mr. Lung's shop? Or could Mrs. Truesdale, by some chance, be part of the smuggling ring?"

CHAPTER XVI

A Chinese Puzzle

"NANCY, that's a good hunch," Ned said. "Let's eavesdrop on Mrs. Truesdale."

Quickly the couple moved up the narrow street and cautiously posted themselves, one on either side, at the door of Mr. Lung's shop.

Nancy and Ned were just in time to see Mrs. Truesdale take a small white paper from her purse. She held it up and turned it first on one side, then the other, for Mr. Lung to see. Then, without looking, she seemingly returned it to her purse. But the paper fluttered to the floor apparently unnoticed.

"Please ship four dozen mah-jongg sets to my sister's gift shop," the woman said to the owner.

Mr. Lung grinned. "Very soon," he said.

Mrs. Truesdale snapped her purse shut and started for the door, evidently unaware that the paper she had shown the man lay on the floor.

"I'd certainly like to see what's written on it," the young sleuth told herself.

"We'd better hide!" Ned warned. He took hold of Nancy's arm and hurried her into the doorway of an adjoining shop.

They saw Mrs. Truesdale come out onto the street, hail a ricksha man, and climb into the cart. As soon as she was out of sight, Nancy urged Ned to return to Mr. Lung's shop with her.

"Suppose you buy a mah-jongg set while I try to find out what is on the paper."

"All right," he agreed.

The eager couple re-entered Mr. Lung's shop. Fortunately, the owner had not noticed the paper. Nancy and Ned smilingly walked up to the counter.

"We decided to come back, as you see," Ned said. "May I see your assortment again?"

The shop owner nodded briefly and turned his back. Nancy quickly leaned down and picked up the paper from the floor. One side was white. Two words were printed on it—Kam Tin.

The girl detective hastily put it in her handbag. By now Mr. Lung had brought out the various sets. Nancy and Ned finally selected one in a teakwood chest.

"Shall I send this to you in the States?" Mr. Lung asked.

Ned had no intention of disclosing their names. "I think we'll take it along," he said.

"I will get your set from stock." Mr. Lung disappeared behind the curtain into his back room. Now was Nancy's chance to take out the paper. This time she noticed that the other side was red. Ned, too, took a glance and both of them gave a slight gasp.

The paper was definitely the cover to a package of firecrackers. On it was painted the fire dragon!

Quickly Nancy put the paper back on the floor. Mr. Lung reappeared and wrapped the set. Ned paid him. Both the young people smiled and thanked the shop owner, then walked outside.

"Where do we go next?" Ned asked.

"Some place where we can talk without being overheard," Nancy whispered.

"Let's go into the lobby of a small hotel near here," he suggested.

As soon as they entered the place, Ned remarked, "This firecracker business seems to prove Mrs. Truesdale *is* part of the dragon gang."

Nancy nodded. "Ned, have you any idea what Kam Tin means? That was printed on the white side of the firecracker paper."

"Why, yes," he replied. "Kam Tin is an ancient Chinese walled city several miles inland in the New Territories, beyond Kowloon."

"I believe," said Nancy, "that Kam Tin is either a place where the smugglers' goods are collected, and perhaps put into the mah-jongg sets, or else it's the spot where Chi Che Soong is a prisoner."

"Oh, I hope it's not the latter!" Ned said. "Why?"

Ned described Kam Tin as hundreds of years behind the times. "There's no plumbing in the one- to two-room houses which are set close together. People and farm animals also are crowded together. The streets are extremely narrow and there's mud everywhere."

"Oh, dear! Poor Chi Che!" Nancy exclaimed.

Ned explained that the men farmed outside the walls. At night the animals were brought inside the city walls for safety.

Nancy was thoughtful for several seconds, then she suggested to Ned that they contact Grandpa Soong's brother as soon as possible. "He's Mr. Lee Soong and is retired now. But at one time he was head of the police in Shanghai."

"Then he's just the one to help," said Ned. "He'll have a personal interest in this case, since Chi Che is involved."

They returned to the Peninsula Hotel lobby and Nancy immediately telephoned Mr. Soong. He asked them to come to his house at once. Nancy, wondering where Mrs. Truesdale was staying, consulted the desk clerk and learned to her delight that the woman was registered at the Peninsula.

"It will be easy to trail her from here," she told Ned.

The two sleuths set off for Mr. Lee Soong's

house. The Chinese was a very handsome man and appeared far younger than his twin brother. He was agile in his movements and spoke quickly and decisively. He was astounded and greatly concerned to hear the details of his great-niece Chi Che's disappearance. At the end of Nancy's recital, he said:

"I shall get in touch with the local police at once and a search will be started for Chi Che. If she is in this crown colony, she will be found. I will work on the case personally, and I beseech you, Miss Drew, to continue your fine efforts."

Nancy promised to do so and said she was going to ask George and Bess to trail Mrs. Truesdale.

Mr. Soong thought this an excellent plan. "Mrs. Truesdale may be the one to lead us to a real solution," he predicted. "I will also have two Chinese detectives follow all three, so no harm will come to the girls."

Nancy thanked him and said she would let him know when her friends started out. She and Ned drove back to the hotel. Mr. Drew had not returned, but Bess and George came in from their shopping tour, arms filled with bundles.

"Oh, this town is fabulous!" Bess exclaimed. "Nancy, wait'll you see what we bought!"

Nancy smiled. "First, though, I want to tell you what Ned and I learned this morning. And I have a sleuthing job for you and George."

When the girls heard about Mrs. Horace

Truesdale, they were thunderstruck. George actually fell into a chair, shocked. "And I thought that woman didn't have a brain in her head!" Bess added.

"If she does belong to the gang," said Nancy, "she might have been the one who sent the faked note and also the flowers to Grandpa Soong at the hospital. The dragon card might even have been meant for me to see so I'd be frightened off the case."

"What do you want Bess and me to do?" George asked eagerly.

"Trail Mrs. Truesdale," Nancy replied. "Or better yet, invite her to go shopping with you and find out everything you possibly can."

"I like that assignment," Bess spoke up quickly. "Get me into a shop and I can stand anything!" George telephoned to Mrs. Truesdale's room and gave the invitation. To the cousins' delight, the woman accepted promptly and said she would be ready to go shopping at two o'clock. Nancy relayed the message to Mr. Soong.

Then, turning to Ned, she asked, "How about you and I going to Kam Tin?"

The young man hesitated. "I'd rather not trust my old car for the trip. But I'd like to go. Suppose we try to charter a helicopter."

"Perfect!" Nancy's eyes sparkled.

Ned drove to the Kai Tak Airport and went inside the building to make arrangements for the flight. Nancy, meanwhile, walked outside and along a fence. Near the control tower was a large Navy helicopter. In the distance she saw a small whirlybird.

"That must be the helicopter Ned and I will take," she figured, and walked toward it. At that moment a small car raced past her and onto the field. In it sat a Chinese man at the wheel, and a girl. She barely caught a glimpse of their faces.

Some distance farther down, the driver stopped the car. The Oriental girl alighted, hurried onto the field, and into a waiting plane. It was a small, two-engine craft. The car whizzed off.

Nancy, lost in thought about the mystery, kept on walking toward the helicopter. Presently she drew near the small craft into which the Chinese girl had hurried. Nancy noticed that there were curtains inside the plane which more than half covered the windows in the passenger compartment. The three landing steps attached to the inside of the door were down.

Suddenly a girl's voice called, "Nancy Drew?"

Nancy was startled and instinctively responded, "Yes." Instantly the Chinese girl peered through the doorway. "Come here!" she said. "I'm Chi Che. I've been a prisoner but I escaped. This pilot is going to fly me to Taipei to get away from the kidnapers. But I want to tell you my whole story first. And, please, how is my grandfather? Poor Grandpa!"

Nancy stared at the girl. She did indeed resemble the photograph of Chi Che Soong. "Hurry!" the girl urged.

Still Nancy hesitated. She wanted to be sure this *was* Chi Che. "But it's not necessary for you to go to Taipei," the young sleuth said finally. "Your uncle is here and knows all about your kidnaping. I'll take you to him and you'll be perfectly safe."

"How do I know you're telling the truth?" the Chinese girl countered. *"Please* come inside a minute. I don't want anybody to see me, but I must give you a message for my grandfather. It is very important."

Nancy turned once more to look for Ned. He was coming on a run. Confident that now she would be all right, the young detective quickly went up the steps and into the plane.

Immediately the door was slammed shut. The pilot pressed the starter buttons on first one, then the other engine. The motors roared to life. At once the plane raced to the nearest runway and took off.

"I don't want to go to Taipei!" Nancy cried out. "Take me back!"

Suddenly the Chinese girl laughed. "My name is Chi Che, but it's not *Chi Che Soong.* Nancy Drew, you're a prisoner!"

CHAPTER XVII

Pursuit of the Sea Furies

As NANCY stood temporarily stunned by her capture, a man peered from behind a curtain where baggage was usually stowed. He was tall and very thin. Nancy had never seen him before, but was sure he was an American.

"How do you do, Miss Drew?" he said triumphantly. "Sorry I didn't meet you in New York, but I've been trailing you and your boy friend around Hong Kong. This chance to take you in our plane is a lucky break. Are you prepared for a long ride?"

Nancy recovered herself and eyed her captors unflinchingly. "You don't think you're going to get away with this, do you?" she retorted.

The Chinese girl and her companion began to laugh scornfully. Then Chi Che said, "She does not know how smart you are, Skinny Kord."

Kord began to taunt Nancy about having her friend George Fayne pose as Chi Che Soong.

"This Chi Che makes a better substitute, doesn't she?"

Nancy ignored the question. "Where is Chi Che Soong?" she demanded.

"In a place where you will never find her," Skinny Kord replied harshly.

He now took a long rope from behind the curtain, and with Chi Che's help, bound Nancy's hands behind her back. He then forced her to lie down across two seats and tied her ankles together.

"You may as well have a nap," Skinny Kord sneered. "You won't be doing any detecting."

He and his girl companion walked up to the front of the plane where the Chinese pilot was gunning the craft to top speed.

"This is a dreadful fix to be in!" Nancy groaned inwardly. "What am I going to do?"

She thought of Ned back at the airport. Had he seen her enter the plane? Would he be able to effect a rescue? "Maybe some other plane will pass us." Nancy's mind raced. "If I could only signal it!"

The young sleuth suddenly remembered the lipstick she was carrying in her skirt pocket. By wriggling and squirming, Nancy was able to pull out the metal tube. By rubbing the case of the lipstick against the rope, she managed to detach the cap. Then she twisted the end until the red stick was showing. Slowly and painfully, Nancy managed to raise herself from the seats.

"I mustn't let anyone see me," she thought.

Keeping her eyes on the pilot's compartment, where her captors were busily talking, Nancy backed up to the window. With the lipstick, she wrote a large SOS backwards on the pane so that it would be legible from the outside. She then drew the small curtains across the window so that the writing would not be seen from inside. Weary from her efforts, the girl detective once more lay down across the two seats.

Meanwhile, back at the airport, Ned Nickerson had arranged to charter the helicopter. He had come from the building and had been surprised to see Nancy go into the small two-engine plane. Then, the next moment, it had suddenly taken off.

"That's strange!" the young man told himself. He dashed back to the airport building and rushed to the control tower to inquire about the plane.

"We know nothing about it except that it came in from Manila last Wednesday," the Chinese controller replied. "It made an unauthorized take-off from the wrong runway before the airfield car could stop it. We tried to attract its attention by a red light from the tower, but the pilot paid no attention. No flight plan whatsoever was filed. They won't answer on the radio."

"So you have no idea of the plane's intention or destination?"

"None whatsoever."

"A friend of mine is on that plane!" Ned cried.

"I'm afraid she's been kidnaped! We must do something at once!"

The official asked Ned several questions. When the youth had identified himself and told enough of the mystery to convince the man a rescue was urgent, the controller called the headquarters of the Fleet Air Arm of the British Royal Navy stationed in Hong Kong harbor. After a lengthy and excited conversation, the official turned to Ned.

"The chase has been started. There's an aircraft carrier a few miles out at sea engaged in practice exercises. It will try to pick up the plane by radar. As soon as it does, fighters will be sent out to force its return. A Navy helicopter is standing by and is just about to leave for the carrier. Would you like to go with it?"

"I sure would!" Ned said.

In a matter of seconds he was on board. The pilot of the helicopter introduced himself as Lieutenant Commander Rawling, commanding officer of one of the Fury Flights.

"Glad to have you aboard," he told Ned. "My boys will be off after that plane shortly. It should still be well within radar range."

Ned sat in the front seat beside the pilot. In a few minutes they had crossed Victoria Island and the great carrier came into view. Three Sea Fury planes took off from its deck, one after the other.

"We'll follow them as quickly as we can," Rawling said, "but this copter is much slower. I'll get

Nancy wrote a large SOS backwards on the pane

the flight leader on the radio." He called and established contact. Ned could hear everything said by both men.

In a few minutes the flight leader reported, "We have the aircraft in sight."

"Close in on him and make him turn back!" Rawling commanded.

"Wilco! Closing on him rapidly now."

Ned heard the flight leader calling the aircraft on the radio, but there was no response.

"They probably hear but won't answer," Ned guessed. "Remember Nancy is on board," he said. "I hope your men won't shoot!"

"No," said Rawling. "They may try to make the pilot think they will, though."

The lieutenant commander gave orders to the Furies, telling them in code the maneuvers to follow. The flight leader called back, "There's an SOS on one of the cabin windows!"

"Nancy must have put that there!" Ned thought excitedly.

In the kidnapers' plane, Nancy was both thrilled and frightened. She watched fascinated as one plane dived in front to slow them down, another swooped below, and the third above. One second she felt she was going to be rescued, the next that she might lose her life; her captors seemed to be desperate enough to perish in the battle.

The Chinese pilot, Skinny Kord, and Chi Che

were talking excitedly both in Cantonese and in English. They had heard every word the commander of the pursuing three-craft squadron had said.

"Why should we take orders from them?" Kord cried out. "We can get away. They'd never risk shooting with Nancy Drew in our plane."

"But we don't dare land in Taipei now or we would be arrested," Chi Che said. "And we may run out of gas and crash if we keep going."

The Chinese pilot said, "If we do not go back, I am not at all sure they will not fire on us. I am not risking it. We are returning."

Since his companions could not fly a plane, they were forced to accede to his decision. In a short time, to Nancy's relief, she felt the craft bank and turn. The pilot had lowered his landing gear as a token of surrender, she later learned.

Nancy pushed her curtains open. Apparently the fighter planes had changed position. Now one flew on each side of the kidnapers' craft, so close that Nancy could see each pilot's face clearly, at least that part of it which was not masked by his helmet and microphone.

Ned was thrilled to hear a new voice calling Kai Tak and asking for landing instructions. "We've won!" he shouted.

He strained his eyes on the distant horizon. Suddenly he pointed. "There they are!"

Four dots rapidly grew in size. Soon the kidnapers' plane came into view with a fighter on either side and one just below.

"We'll follow them in," Rawling said. He radioed the airport for police to be on hand. As soon as the mystery plane had set down, the fighter leader landed, but instructed the others to return to the carrier. The helicopter was on the ground in seconds.

The police were just handcuffing the arrested trio when Ned dashed into the aircraft. "Nancy!" He unfastened her bonds.

"Oh, Ned, how can I ever thank you for rescuing me!" she cried. "I admit I've never been more scared in my life."

"How do you feel now?" he asked solicitously.

"I feel fine—really I do."

"Thank goodness!" Ned said.

None of the prisoners would talk, so Nancy related as much of their story as she knew. Then the three captives were taken away.

The young people said good-by to Lieutenant Commander Rawling and thanked him profusely. Nancy and Ned then walked to the airport building, where Nancy washed her face and hands, combed her hair, and rested for a short time. Then she told Ned she was ready to go on to Kam Tin.

The young man shook his head in astonishment. "You can certainly take it!" he said admiringly.

Ned found that the Chinese helicopter pilot, Jimmy Ching, was still available. Soon Nancy and Ned were air-borne, heading for Kam Tin.

It was not a long ride and soon the helicopter was hovering over the walled city. It looked like a toy city surrounded by a moat. Beyond lay a vast expanse of fields with a farmhouse here and there.

The whirlybird came down on a field and the occupants alighted. As the visitors began walking through the ancient city, the inhabitants stared at them expressionlessly.

The three proceeded up one alley and down another. They could easily look into the houses, which were all open to the roadways and had bamboo curtains. These were now raised, but the pilot said they were lowered at night. Nancy and her fellow searchers saw nothing to indicate any smuggling activities, or that Chi Che Soong was being held prisoner in Kam Tin.

Nancy observed, as they walked along, that the walled city was crowded and unsanitary. Nevertheless, she was intrigued by an artistic religious custom of the inhabitants. On walls, both inside and outside the homes, were brackets holding candles, flowers, and incense. The candles were lighted and the incense gave off a fragrant aroma.

"I don't think the people of Kam Tin have anything to do with the mystery of the fire dragon," Ned whispered to Nancy presently. "The paper Mrs. Truesdale showed Mr. Lung might refer to some farmhouse in the area instead of a place in town."

Nancy nodded. The trio went through the city gate and set off down the main road toward the nearest farmhouse. As they approached it, the three could hear rhythmic hammering. The sound was not noisy; on the contrary, it was muffled and pleasant.

"That hammering reminds me of goldbeaters," Ned remarked.

As Nancy and her companions drew closer to the farmhouse, they suddenly noticed a car coming in the opposite direction. It turned abruptly into a lane which led to the house. "Let's hide and see if we can find out what's going on here," Nancy suggested.

They managed to conceal themselves behind a shed a few feet from the house. The driver of the car was talking to a Chinese farmer.

Ned translated, "Is the shipment ready?"

The farmer replied, "Yes."

The driver then asked, "You kept enough to pay for the work?"

The farmer replied angrily, "I cannot use this. I want Hong Kong dollars."

The argument went on. The farmer threatened to expose the caller to the authorities if he were not paid at once. Finally the driver pulled out a wad of bills and handed it to the farmer.

The farmer pocketed the money, then called to

someone inside the house. Several Chinese men, carrying two heavy chests, came outside and put them in the car. The caller drove off.

"I'm sure we have a clue to the smuggling!" Nancy whispered. "We'd better get back to the airport as fast as we can!"

Her companions agreed. As soon as they reached Kai Tak, the girl detective telephoned Mr. Lee Soong and told him of the Kam Tin trip, giving the car's license number and a description of the driver.

"I will arrange to have the police find this driver and trail him," Mr. Soong said. "And the farmhouse at Kam Tin will be searched."

Nancy thanked him. "I can hardly wait to find out what happens," she told Mr. Soong excitedly.

CHAPTER XVIII

A New Assignment

THE ex-police chief, Mr. Lee Soong, chuckled. "Impatience," he said, "is like a goat butting its head aimlessly on the wall. All he does is mar the wall and wear himself out."

Nancy laughed. "How true that is!" she replied. "I will try to be patient, but I shall have my mind on the case every minute until I hear from you."

Mr. Soong said it probably would be hours before there would be any police report on the suspicious farmer and the man who had taken away the heavy boxes.

When Nancy told this to Ned, he said, "In the meantime, how about our having some fun? We'll do a little sight-seeing with Bess and George and your father."

"I'd love it." Nancy twinkled. "Is it some place special?"

Ned nodded. "I thought we'd take in the Chinese opera for a while, then go on to eat at a houseboat restaurant out near the little village of Aberdeen. You will be amazed at that place," he added. "I shan't tell you any more about it."

Nancy smiled. "You know the only way you could get me to stop working on one mystery is to intrigue me with another. Now I can't wait to see Aberdeen."

Mr. Drew, Bess, and George had not returned, so Nancy and Ned left a note explaining their plan. Then the couple set off by ferry for Hong Kong to attend the Chinese opera.

"It goes on for hours and hours," Ned told his companion. "Whole families attend, even with their small babies. It is like an indoor picnic, so far as the audience goes."

Later, as they entered the very large ornate theater, Nancy knew what Ned meant. Small children and adults were moving up and down the aisles. Food vendors seemed to be everywhere and many people were eating picnic suppers. Infants lay asleep in a mother's or grandmother's arms, while the older people and the teen-age group tried to concentrate on the show.

In contrast to the plain dress and noisiness of the audience, the production was most dignified and elaborate. Nancy stared in fascination at the exquisitely embroidered silk and satin costumes and the lofty headdresses worn by the players.

Each actor moved about the stage slowly and a bit woodenly. But there was grace and charm to the performance.

"It seems to me," Nancy whispered to Ned, "that the audience isn't paying too much attention. Why?"

Ned explained that the Chinese like to see the same plays over and over. Many of them practically knew the scores by heart.

"Even though they don't keep their eyes on the stage every minute, and can even converse or move about, they still know everything that is going on," Ned told her.

Half an hour later, he said, "Let's go now."

It was growing dark as Ned hailed a taxi to take them to Aberdeen. "It's the oldest village of the fishermen of Hong Kong Island," he explained. "Families live on the junks and even in the small sampans."

When they reached the water front of Aberdeen, Nancy stared in wonder. "Why, it's almost a city of boats—of all sizes!" she cried.

"Yes," Ned said, adding that the residents jumped from craft to craft when they wanted to go ashore.

"But they spend most of their time on the water," he added. "The junks go out for deep-sea fishing, but the sampans stay around here. The women and children remain on them while the men are at work. The women are good oarsmen, and take their boats everywhere. Out there in the harbor are a floating church and a floating school."

"How fascinating!" Nancy exclaimed.

"We'll hire one of the sampans," Ned said. "It's the only way to reach the floating restaurant." He pointed off in the distance where they could see a long boat brilliantly lighted.

"There are several others, but I think we'll go to the Sea Palace," Ned added.

Several women were already calling to the couple, offering to take them. Ned finally signaled a mother and daughter with whom he had ridden before. They smiled as Nancy and Ned stepped down into the sampan and walked into the arched open-front cabin at the rear.

As they left the dock, Nancy was amazed at the strength of the two women propelling their boat. Both were short and very slight, probably weighing not more than ninety pounds. Yet they seemed to have muscles of steel as they stood so straight and rotated their heavy oars through the water.

Upon reaching the Sea Palace, Nancy and Ned climbed a stairway to the deck. They walked around to the far side where a group of people were leaning over the rail and pointing below.

"See those boats down there?" Ned asked.

Nancy had never seen anything like them. They had compartments of water in which live fish and shellfish were swimming around.

"You pick your dinner alive," the young man said, laughing.

Fishermen below were recommending the various native fish. Nancy sighed. "I wouldn't know one fish from another," she confessed. "I shall leave the entire dinner to your judgment, Ned."

"Good!" he said, and guided her inside the restaurant.

The headwaiter told them there were no small tables left. "Do you mind sitting at a larger one?" he inquired. Ned said they would not, and they were escorted to one near a window.

"First we'll have bacon and cucumber soup," Ned told the waiter. "Then some stewed shrimp." He looked up at Nancy to see if she approved. When she nodded, he went on, "A little sweet-and-sour pork, beef fried in oyster sauce, bamboo shoots, rice, and almond tea."

Nancy laughed. "This sounds like a Chinese Thanksgiving dinner. I'm not sure I can eat so much." Ned assured her that the portions would not be large.

The couple finished the delectable soup and were busy with the stewed shrimp when Nancy happened to look toward the entrance door.

"Ned!" she said tensely. "Here comes Mrs. Truesdale with a Chinese escort! He's not Mr. Lung, though."

Ned turned to look. The headwaiter led the

newcomers to a table some distance up the long room. Mrs. Truesdale did not notice Nancy and her companion.

Ned suddenly grinned. "Mrs. Truesdale's shadows are right behind her!"

Nancy's eyes widened. Bess and George, looking extremely weary, entered the room. As they began to follow Mrs. Truesdale, Nancy quickly got out of her chair and went after the girls.

"You!" Bess exclaimed.

"Come join us and enjoy yourselves for a while," Nancy invited. "I can see you've really been on the job."

"Have we!" George laughed. "That Truesdale woman has nine lives when it comes to energy. We've been shopping everywhere with her today, and we decided to keep trailing her this evening."

The two girls dropped exhausted into seats at the table with Nancy and Ned. They had hardly had time to put napkins in their laps when a nice-looking Chinese man hurried up to them. He paused a moment to whisper to George:

"I'll take over. Get some rest." He went on, and without waiting to be seated, pulled out a chair at the table next to Mrs. Truesdale. From this vantage point, the others knew, he could overhear every word of her conversation.

"Who is he?" Ned asked George.

"I don't know, but he trailed us all afternoon."

Nancy said he must be one of the detectives

whom Mr. Soong had retained to follow the girls. "If he isn't, the real sleuth will doubtless be following him, so in any case I think you girls can relax."

"Thank goodness!" said Bess. "My feet hurt and I'm absolutely starved."

The others laughed. Then Ned repeated the menu he had ordered for himself and Nancy. "Would you girls like the same?"

Bess and George agreed to try the exotic dishes. As Nancy and her friends ate the delicious meal, the group exchanged stories. George reported that Mrs. Truesdale had neither said nor done anything the least bit suspicious.

Bess declared, "I don't see how she can be connected with the mystery."

"Of course I have nothing to go on except what happened in Mr. Lung's shop," Nancy remarked.

Bess and George were completely astounded to hear of Nancy's capture, of her rescue, of her trip to Kam Tin with Ned, and of its results.

"You had enough adventure today to do me for a lifetime," Bess complained. "And this mystery is far from solved. Goodness only knows what'll happen next."

Bess's worries did not seem to affect her appetite and she was able to eat every crumb of the food brought to her. George and Nancy declined dessert, but Bess and Ned ate custard pudding dotted with almonds.

When they finished, George said to Nancy, "Do you think we should stay until Mrs. Truesdale leaves, so we can follow her?"

"No," Nancy replied. "I'm sure the police will trail her. We had all better get a good night's sleep."

When they reached the hotel, Nancy found a message that she was to telephone Mr. Lee Soong as soon as she came in. Nancy called him at once. Mr. Soong said he had several things to report to the young sleuth.

"First, the police were not able to locate the man who left the farmhouse with the heavy boxes. We think someone saw you and Mr. Nickerson leaving the place and warned him to disappear.

"We did raid the farmhouse and found that the owner and his workmen have been beating gold objects of all kinds into small flat pieces. We believe that these have been smuggled out of the country inside various containers."

"Mah-jongg sets!" Nancy exclaimed.

"Possibly," Mr. Soong agreed. "Every one of the goldbeaters insisted he was innocent of any wrongdoing. They finally admitted they thought something illegal was being done with the gold, but did not know what."

Mr. Soong went on to say that a police guard had been placed at the farmhouse to seize any suspicious callers. "No one has come there yet," he said, "but the police uncovered a great many gold objects, which probably were stolen from shops and homes and brought there to be beaten into small pieces."

The Chinese now changed the subject and invited Nancy and her friends to attend a big garden party to be given by a relative of his. "The party will be held tomorrow evening. Special fireworks will be displayed and I'm sure you will enjoy them. You have probably guessed that I am about to ask you to do a little detective work while there."

"I will be glad to," said Nancy eagerly.

Mr. Soong said that at his request his friend had invited several special guests. "They may or may not be involved in the mystery we are all trying to solve. You know two of them—Mrs. Truesdale and Mr. Lung."

Nancy could hear the ex-police chief give a sigh of hope. "Anyhow, it is just possible my twin brother's wish will be realized during the party. But the police require the help of you and your friends. Will Miss George Fayne please come looking as much like my niece as possible?"

"I am sure she will be happy to," Nancy responded.

"That is very fine," Mr. Soong said. "I will meet you at the hotel as darkness falls."

Nancy would have liked to hear more, but Mr. Soong divulged nothing further. She thanked him for the invitation and accepted it with alacrity.

CHAPTER XIX

Symbolic Fireworks

MR. DREW came in so late during the evening that Nancy did not see him until the following morning at breakfast. At her request the meal was served in the living room of their suite. After the waiter had left, the girls brought the lawyer up to date on the happenings of the day before.

He looked at Nancy intently. "Thank goodness you're safe, my dear. I suppose there is no use asking you to give up work on this case, now that it seems so near a solution."

Nancy smiled. "Of course you know the answer would be no." Then she told him about the invitation to the party that evening and how Mr. Lee Soong hoped there would be another break in the mystery. "Will you be able to go with us?" she asked.

The lawyer shook his head. "My assignment here has proved to be a tough one, and tonight I must confer with the disagreeing heirs. But I too hope to get a break in the case by tomorrow."

"I suppose there won't be any detective work for us today, Nancy?" Ned asked.

"I can't think of any before tonight." Nancy smiled.

"Then let's all do some sight-seeing. First thing I know," the young man said ruefully, "your father and you will wind up your cases and fly back to New York without having seen half the interesting things around here."

George asked Ned what he had in mind. "You most certainly should take the tramway up Victoria Peak. Then we'll drive out to Chung Chi College. I want you to meet some of the fellows. We'll have lunch with them and then go to the international volleyball game between the United States and Japan against Free China and India."

"It sounds very exciting," Nancy answered.

Bess smiled, her dimples deep. She did not say what the others thought she was going to; that the date sounded entrancing. Instead, she asked, "Ned, I wish you could straighten me out on something. I've been so busy sleuthing since I reached this place, I haven't figured out the political setup."

Ned laughed. "There are plenty of people who have lived here a long time and still don't understand it," he said. "But actually it is quite simple. The whole area is a British crown colony.

"Hong Kong Island was ceded to the British when the Treaty of Nanking was signed in 1842. Then, in 1860, through the Convention of Peking, a tip of Kowloon Peninsula was added, as well as small Stonecutters' Island.

"In 1898 more land was added to the colony. It was leased for ninety-nine years and became known as the New Territories. It includes the rest of Kowloon Peninsula and the hundred and ninety-eight islands in adjacent waters."

"Thank you, Professor Nickerson." Bess leaned back in her chair. "I'll try to remember all that!"

"One interesting thing I've learned," said Ned, "is that the word Kowloon means 'nine dragons.' It is named for the range of hills behind the city. In fact, it separates the city from the New Territories."

George grinned. "We can't get away from the dragons! Any more interesting stories?"

Ned laughed. "After that crack, I'm not sure I should tell you. But here is one. Out in the harbor there is an island called Lantao. On it live barking deer."

The others broke into laughter and accused Ned of spoofing. But the young man insisted he was not. "If you'll stay long enough, I'll take you over there and you can hear them."

Later, the girls and Ned started their ride up Victoria Peak on the tramway. They found it an exciting experience. The cable car stopped at stations on various levels, to let local residents get on or alight.

Streets stretched out in all directions on the steep mountainside, and houses nestled firmly among the rocks. The view from the top was magnificent and the girls could take in at a glance the enormous and bustling population on both land and water.

When they descended to the foot of the peak, the sight-seers returned by ferry to the Peninsula Hotel and drove to Ned's college. The girls were greatly impressed. All the buildings were new and stood on top of a hill. In a valley to one side were the very large athletic fields.

When they pulled into the parking area, two young Chinese came to meet them. Ned introduced the handsome boys as friends of his. "Charlie Tsang, and this is Philip Ming."

The two young men bowed low, then said they had arranged to eat luncheon with them in a private dining room usually reserved for faculty members. During the meal there was a constant flow of amusing banter among the young people. The Chinese students spoke excellent English and seemed to understand American slang and humor.

But finally the conversation took a serious turn when Charlie asked, "Ned, I do not wish to pry into your private affairs, but what have you been doing in Hong Kong recently?"

Ned grinned. "Just look at my companions and see for yourself," he said.

"This is no joke," Philip Ming spoke up. "Charlie and I were called from class to the president's office yesterday afternoon. He told us two men had been here inquiring about you, Ned. They thought you should be ordered back to the college immediately because you were a menace in town."

The Americans were astonished. "A menace!" Nancy cried out. "What do they mean?"

"I cannot imagine," Charlie replied. "These same people also said that Ned's mixed up in a smuggling racket, and that he's being misled by unscrupulous persons. However, the individuals do not want to prefer any charges against you, Ned, but requested that the president insist you be made to remain here at college and not go into town."

Ned and the girls were more astounded than ever. They now told the two Chinese young men a little about the case on which they had been working.

Nancy expressed the opinion that the two visitors to the college were part of the smuggling ring. "Naturally they'd feel Ned is becoming a 'menace' to them, and want him out of their way."

Ned suddenly laughed upon hearing this. "So I'm that important, am I?" he asked.

"I'll say you are!" George spoke up. "Nancy

needs a bodyguard. In fact, I'd say she needs more than one."

At once Charlie and Philip offered to help. When Ned insisted he could do the job alone, the two boys turned to Bess and George. "Do you not need protection, too?" Charlie asked. "This evening perhaps? We would like to take you sight-seeing."

Both Bess and George said they thought it would be fun but that they had promised to meet Mr. Soong. "Could we make it tomorrow evening?" George suggested.

"Tomorrow evening it is," Philip agreed and Charlie nodded.

The young people next attended the volleyball game. They followed the contest with increasing excitement as first one side, then the other, went ahead in score. In the end the United States and Japan won over Free China and India.

As the visitors were ready to leave in Ned's car, Bess declared, "This has been a lucky day!"

"And we hope the luck will continue," Philip Ming said as he and Charlie bowed.

"Thank you." Bess smiled. She was thinking, "Oh, I hope we will be lucky this evening and solve the mystery of Chi Che Soong!"

When Ned dropped Nancy and her friends at the hotel, saying he would see them later, the girls went at once to one of the shops there to pick out a Chinese costume for George. As soon as dinner was over, they changed into their party clothes. Nancy and Bess helped George disguise herself as Chi Che.

She had just finished applying make-up when the telephone rang. Mr. Lee Soong was calling Nancy to say that two taxis were waiting. He requested that George come downstairs alone, and casually hold a scarf so that her face would be partially covered.

"Miss Drew," Mr. Soong went on, "ask your friend to bow to me, and act in every way as if she were Chinese, and indeed my great-niece. She and I will take the first taxi. Will the rest of you follow in the other?"

"Certainly," said Nancy. "We will be down immediately."

"That is excellent." Mr. Soong added, "It is my great hope that someone at the party tonight will be startled upon seeing Miss Fayne's disguise and reveal a clue as to where Chi Che is."

Ned joined the girls and a short time later the two taxis drew up at the gate of a beautiful estate facing the harbor. Hundreds of lighted lanterns hung from among the trees in the gardens, and haunting Chinese music was being played.

The group alighted. As Mr. Soong and George walked on ahead, Bess whispered to Nancy, "George seems even more convincing as Chi Che than she did in New York." Nancy nodded in agreement.

Presently the guests heard firecrackers being set off. "That means the celebrations are about to begin," Ned explained. "Every Chinese function starts with firecrackers."

"Let's go watch," Bess urged.

There were many paths and little arched bridges over ponds and brooks. One of the paths, which everyone seemed to be following, led through an attractively carved, horseshoe-shaped arch. Beyond, in the center of a clearing, Nancy and her friends could see a series of large metal frames for the display pieces of the fireworks.

All the guests had gathered to observe the display. George was alone, having preceded Mr. Soong. Among the onlookers just ahead was Mrs. Truesdale! The ex-police chief spread out his arms. Nancy sensed that Mr. Soong's move might be a signal for her group to separate, and suggested that she, Bess, and Ned take up different positions nearby. She herself remained at the rear in back of the arch.

Some of the fireworks were in the form of floral pieces, one more beautiful than the other. Finally the center one was set off. As one section after another of it blazed into the night sky, Nancy gasped.

It was a huge fire dragon!

"It is magnificent, but frightening!" the girl detective thought.

Nancy glanced about to see Bess's and Ned's reactions. She could not discern her friends in the crowd ahead of her. But her gaze fastened on something else that almost made her heart stop beating.

Mr. Stromberg was sneaking up behind Mr. Soong. Was he going to attack the Chinese?

At that very instant George stood in the full glare of the fire dragon. Mrs. Truesdale turned and stared at the girl. She suddenly shrieked: "Chi Che! You got off the junk!"

Nancy's attention had been diverted for the moment from the scene nearer her. Now she saw that Mr. Stromberg was about to strike Mr. Soong. At the same instant, Ned appeared from among some bushes and leaped on the bookstore owner.

Swiftly Nancy started toward Mrs. Truesdale, but advanced only three feet. Someone behind her clapped a hand over the girl's mouth and, with strong arms, dragged her away.

Nancy struggled and fought, but to no avail. The man who had seized her was suddenly aided by another, who lifted up her feet.

As she was carried off, the girl detective became aware that a Eurasian woman was accompanying the two men. Her strange captors took a path which was isolated and almost dark. No one came to Nancy's rescue.

CHAPTER XX

The Escape

As THE great fireworks dragon continued to crackle and emit fire and smoke, George and Bess dashed forward and grabbed Mrs. Truesdale.

"Take your hands off me!" the woman ordered.

At that moment Mr. Lee Soong and Ned came forward dragging Mr. Stromberg. The ex-police chief told the prisoners, "As you Americans say, I think your little game is up."

"What on earth are you talking about?" Mrs. Truesdale asked airily. "Just because I said something to this impostor? I don't know why she's dressed up like a Chinese. For a moment I thought she was a wash-amah I know named Chi Che. She works for a friend of mine."

By this time most of the guests had gathered around. Four men pushed their way through the crowd, nodded to Mr. Soong, and took charge of the two prisoners.

"These men belong to the colony police," Mr. Soong explained.

"This is an outrage!" Mrs. Truesdale screamed. "I am just a tourist, not a criminal."

All this time Mr. Stromberg had been glaring at Bess and George. Finally he said, "Officer, you have made a great mistake. Mrs. Truesdale and I have been friends a long time, and would swear to the honesty of each other."

George faced the man squarely. "If you are honest, why did you run away from your bookshop? And where are you keeping Chi Che Soong?"

"I can only guess what you're talking about," Mr. Stromberg said icily. "A girl named Chi Che Soong worked in my bookshop for a short while. I understand she has disappeared, but why should I know where she is?"

"Take these people away!" Mr. Soong ordered the detectives.

As the group moved off, Bess suddenly asked, "Where's Nancy?"

"She was standing by that archway back there when the trouble started," said Ned.

Mr. Soong and the young people searched the estate gardens thoroughly. Nancy was not in sight.

Bess closed her eyes in terror. "I just know the gang has kidnaped Nancy again!"

The worried group held a conference. Ned said, "Mrs. Truesdale mentioned that Chi Che was on a junk. Perhaps that's where members of the gang took Nancy. Have you any suggestions on how to find that junk?" he asked Mr. Soong.

The Chinese thought a moment, then said, "Mr. Lung recently acquired a combination sail-and-motor junk. I will try to find out where he keeps it."

Mr. Soong hurried off but was back in a few minutes. He had not only obtained the information by telephone but had received permission from their hostess to use her motor launch for a chase.

"Please to follow me," the Chinese requested.

At that very moment Nancy was being pushed aboard the large, sumptuous junk. Quickly the pilot cast off and the powerful motors began to move the craft toward the sea. A handkerchief which had been stuffed into Nancy's mouth was now removed, but she was warned by her captors not to make a sound or her life would be in danger.

At that instant Nancy caught sight of a Chinese girl prisoner kneeling in the roofed-over section at the rear of the junk. From the photograph she had seen in New York, she was sure this was the real Chi Che Soong!

"Let your prisoner go at once!" Nancy demanded. "And me too."

Her captors paid no attention and shoved Nancy toward the Chinese girl. But they did untie their prisoners. In a very low tone Nancy introduced herself and told Chi Che how she herself had become involved in the mystery.

"I heard the gang talking about you," the Chinese girl whispered. "Mr. Breen took my keys. He came back to the apartment house and from the hall overheard your aunt telephoning you to come and solve the mystery. He was frightened away by the arrival of the superintendent."

Chi Che now began to relate the amazing story which had led to her capture.

"One day when I was in the bookshop I overheard Mr. Stromberg talking on the phone. I realized he was part of a gang smuggling gold from Hong Kong into the United States. Small pieces were hidden inside the ivories and in the chests of mah-jongg sets."

Chi Che also confirmed Nancy's other suspicions that Mrs. Truesdale, Mr. Stromberg, and Mr. Lung were the ringleaders. Because of Mr. Lung's name the group had adopted the dragon as a password.

"Was the owner of the stationery-and-gift shop in Chinatown a member of the gang?" Nancy asked.

"No, he is innocent."

The Chinese girl said that after she had heard the phone conversation at the bookshop about the smuggling, she had not known what to do. "I decided to go home and talk to my grandfather about it. When I arrived, he was not there. I assumed he had gone out walking as he often did. . . . Nancy, how is my grandfather? This must have been a dreadful shock to him."

Nancy told Chi Che about the stolen manuscript but skipped lightly over the fact that Grandpa Soong was in the hospital and not very well.

Chi Che caught her breath. "I must have mentioned the manuscript to Mr. Stromberg. How unfortunate!"

"Please tell me just how you were captured," Nancy requested.

"While I was in the apartment trying to decide what to do, our buzzer sounded. I opened the door, thinking Grandpa had forgotten his key. A strange man pushed his way in and warned me to keep still. The man, who I later learned was named Breen, said Mr. Stromberg knew I had overheard his phone conversation about the smuggling."

"He is in jail," Nancy told her. "Also two men nicknamed Ryle and Smitty."

Chi Che went on to tell how Breen, at gun point, had made her write the letter to Grandpa Soong on stationery which he had brought.

"Fortunately, there were two sheets," the Chinese girl explained. "While Breen was pacing around—I suppose he was looking for the manuscript—he did not notice that I was writing the note to your aunt on the second sheet. But he told me to hurry up. I handed him the note for my grandfather, and while he turned his back a moment to put it in a prominent place, I slipped the other note under the adjoining door to Miss Drew's apartment."

Chi Che said she had then been taken to Mrs. Truesdale's apartment and heavily guarded. Stromberg had tried to throw suspicion away from himself by his early-morning call at the Soong apartment. If anyone had answered the door, he would have said that he had come to find out if Chi Che was going to return to her job at the bookshop.

"When you and your kind friends and the police seemed to be nearing a solution to the mystery," Chi Che continued, "my captors took me one night on a private plane going to Hong Kong. When we arrived, they brought me aboard this junk.

"We've been on the water most of the time, just putting in to shore once in a while for supplies and messages. Nancy, your capture was all planned this evening. Some of the smugglers sneaked into the party."

Nancy now told of the imminent capture of Mr. Stromberg and Mrs. Truesdale just as she herself was dragged away. "Chi Che, we must escape from here. Can you swim?"

"Yes, I can."

The young sleuth gave directions on how the

girls would proceed. "Let's stroll out on deck. When there's a sampan not far away, I'll give the signal. We'll climb onto the side, and dive in together. We'll head for the sampan."

The two girls separated, Nancy going outside first. She drew in great breaths of fresh air and stretched as if weary from her cramped position. Chi Che followed and kept her eyes glued on the other girl. The woman and the men on board paid little attention to them.

Suddenly Nancy gave the signal. The two girls kicked off their shoes, leaped up to the top of the wooden side of the junk, and dived in. The woman on board screamed and at once the men rushed to the side.

Nancy and Chi Che were swimming toward the passing sampan as fast as they could. They reached it at the same time and pulled themselves aboard.

The women manning it cried out in astonishment. Quickly Chi Che assured them in their native tongue that they would not be harmed. She said that the girls must get to shore immediately.

"Ch'ing hao."—"Please okay," the older woman said. She and her companion began to paddle furiously and fifteen minutes later Nancy and Chi Che were safe on land.

"I must get to a phone at once," Nancy said.

Chi Che translated this to the women and the younger one led them to a small shop which was still open. Smiling, Chi Che asked for her name and promised to pay the next day for the boat ride.

As she went off, Chi Che explained to the shop owner the reason for the girls' bedraggled appearance. He looked startled but took them to the telephone in the back room. Nancy at once put in a call to the hotel, hoping that her father had returned.

Hearing his voice, she cried in relief, "Oh, Dad! Chi Che Soong is with me. We just swam the bay to get away from some of the smugglers. They're on Mr. Lung's junk. I was captured and taken aboard. I'll be right home, but do what you can to round up those kidnapers."

"You poor child!" the lawyer exclaimed. "Get here as fast as you can. In the meantime, I'll follow through."

During this conversation, Chi Che had been talking with the shop owner about getting transportation to the hotel. He said the girls were on the Kowloon Peninsula at a small town some distance from the city. "I will see what I can do."

The helpful, excited man hurried to the street. He was gone for several minutes, then the girls saw him riding up in a dilapidated car.

A young Chinese man sat at the wheel. He smiled at the girls and said in English, "Please to pardon my old jalopy. I will be glad to take you to the hotel."

When they reached the hotel, Nancy asked the driver to wait while she went upstairs to get money to pay him for his trouble, but the young man refused to accept any payment. "I am very happy to help you. From what I hear, you have solved a great mystery and benefited our colony. I am only a humble citizen, but I thank you."

The girls smiled and hopped from the car. They waved as he went off, then hurried into the hotel and up to the Drews' suite. As they reached the door to the living room, it opened wide. Nancy's father clasped her in his arms. Then she broke away to introduce Chi Che not only to him but to Bess, George, and Ned. Mr. Lee Soong greeted his great-niece in Cantonese.

Nancy was hugged and bombarded with questions. Mr. Drew held up his hand. "Both these swimmers must take hot showers and put on dry clothes before they tell their story," he insisted.

Chi Che was given the suit which George had worn to the party. When she put it on and combed her hair, there was indeed a striking resemblance between her and George!

"I have a fine American twin," she said, smiling.

"This is part of the way we solved the mystery of the fire dragon," Bess told her with a chuckle.

When the girls returned to the living room, stories were quickly exchanged. Nancy and Chi Che were thrilled to learn from Mr. Soong that he and Ned and some of the colony police had arrived at Mr. Lung's junk soon after the girls had dived overboard.

"We caught all the men and the woman before they had a chance to get away," the ex-police chief explained. "And also the man who drove off with the chests from Kam Tin. In them were mah-jongg sets containing hidden gold. Mr. Lung and several others who worked for the smugglers are also in jail."

Presently Nancy said, "All of us here are so overjoyed that Chi Che has been found, I suggest we telephone overseas to Grandpa Soong and share the good news."

The others nodded. Before Nancy could put in the call to the hospital in New York, the telephone rang. The police had a message for Mr. Lee Soong —his brother's stolen manuscript had been found in Mr. Lung's shop. It was now in the possession of the police.

Mr. Lung had confessed that it had been stolen from the New York apartment by Reilley Moot for Mr. Stromberg, Mrs. Truesdale, Breen, and himself as a private project outside the smuggling ring. Ryle, knowing the combination of Mr. Stromberg's safe, had tried to double-cross his friends by taking the manuscript, but later had been caught by them. The others, unable to dispose of the manuscript themselves in Hong Kong, had asked Mr. Lung to try selling it.

The overseas call was put through and soon Grandpa Soong was saying, "Chi Che! I can hardly believe it! You are safe?"

When Chi Che told him the stolen manuscript had been recovered, the others could hear his gasp of astonishment and delight. When he and his granddaughter finished talking, Grandpa Soong asked to speak to Nancy.

"I am such a happy man," he said. "And I must thank you for everything—you and your kind friends. If you'll permit me to do so, I will dedicate my book to you three girls."

Nancy was touched and said she could not imagine any greater reward for her efforts.

"Grandpa Soong, will you do me a great favor?" she asked. "Please get in touch with my aunt and tell her the good news."

"I will do that at once," Mr. Soong promised.

As Nancy turned from the telephone, she felt as if she had lost something. For a second the young detective looked about her. Then she realized why she felt this way. The mystery of the fire dragon had been solved—there was nothing more for her to do! But Nancy was sure that soon another case would come along. It proved to be *The Clue of the Dancing Puppet.*

Nancy's eyes sparkled. Then she said to the others, "Dad told me a few minutes ago that he too has won his case. So all's well that ends well!"

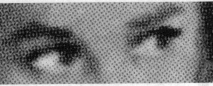

Match Wits with The Hardy Boys®!

Collect the Complete
Hardy Boys Mystery Stories®
by Franklin W. Dixon

#1: The Tower Treasure
#2: The House on the Cliff
#3: The Secret of the Old Mill
#4: The Missing Chums
#5: Hunting for Hidden Gold
#6: The Shore Road Mystery
#7: The Secret of the Caves
#8: The Mystery of Cabin Island
#9: The Great Airport Mystery
#10: What Happened at Midnight
#11: While the Clock Ticked
#12: Footprints Under the Window
#13: The Mark on the Door
#14: The Hidden Harbor Mystery
#15: The Sinister Signpost
#16: A Figure in Hiding
#17: The Secret Warning
#18: The Twisted Claw
#19: The Disappearing Floor
#20: The Mystery of the Flying Express
#21: The Clue of the Broken Blade
#22: The Flickering Torch Mystery
#23: The Melted Coins
#24: The Short-Wave Mystery
#25: The Secret Panel
#26: The Phantom Freighter
#27: The Secret of Skull Mountain
#28: The Sign of the Crooked Arrow
#29: The Secret of the Lost Tunnel
#30: The Wailing Siren Mystery
#31: The Secret of Wildcat Swamp
#32: The Crisscross Shadow
#33: The Yellow Feather Mystery

#34: The Hooded Hawk Mystery
#35: The Clue in the Embers
#36: The Secret of Pirates' Hill
#37: The Ghost at Skeleton Rock
#38: The Mystery at Devil's Paw
#39: The Mystery of the Chinese Junk
#40: Mystery of the Desert Giant
#41: The Clue of the Screeching Owl
#42: The Viking Symbol Mystery
#43: The Mystery of the Aztec Warrior
#44: The Haunted Fort
#45: The Mystery of the Spiral Bridge
#46: The Secret Agent on Flight 101
#47: Mystery of the Whale Tattoo
#48: The Arctic Patrol Mystery
#49: The Bombay Boomerang
#50: Danger on Vampire Trail
#51: The Masked Monkey
#52: The Shattered Helmet
#53: The Clue of the Hissing Serpent
#54: The Mysterious Caravan
#55: The Witchmaster's Key
#56: The Jungle Pyramid
#57: The Firebird Rocket
#58: The Sting of the Scorpion
#59: Night of the Werewolf
#60: Mystery of the Samurai Sword
#61: The Pentagon Spy
#62: The Apeman's Secret
#63: The Mummy Case
#64: Mystery of Smugglers Cove
#65: The Stone Idol
#66: The Vanishing Thieves

The Hardy Boys Back-to-Back
#1: The Tower Treasure/#2: The House on the Cliff

Celebrate over 70 Years with the World's Greatest Super Sleuths!

Match Wits with Super Sleuth Nancy Drew!

Collect the Complete
Nancy Drew Mystery Stories®
by Carolyn Keene

#1: The Secret of the Old Clock
#2: The Hidden Staircase
#3: The Bungalow Mystery
#4: The Mystery at Lilac Inn
#5: The Secret of Shadow Ranch
#6: The Secret of Red Gate Farm
#7: The Clue in the Diary
#8: Nancy's Mysterious Letter
#9: The Sign of the Twisted Candles
#10: Password to Larkspur Lane
#11: The Clue of the Broken Locket
#12: The Message in the Hollow Oak
#13: The Mystery of the Ivory Charm
#14: The Whispering Statue
#15: The Haunted Bridge
#16: The Clue of the Tapping Heels
#17: The Mystery of the Brass-Bound Trunk
#18: The Mystery of the Moss-Covered Mansion
#19: The Quest of the Missing Map
#20: The Clue in the Jewel Box
#21: The Secret in the Old Attic
#22: The Clue in the Crumbling Wall
#23: The Mystery of the Tolling Bell
#24: The Clue in the Old Album
#25: The Ghost of Blackwood Hall
#26: The Clue of the Leaning Chimney
#27: The Secret of the Wooden Lady
#28: The Clue of the Black Keys
#29: Mystery at the Ski Jump
#30: The Clue of the Velvet Mask
#31: The Ringmaster's Secret
#32: The Scarlet Slipper Mystery

#33: The Witch Tree Symbol
#34: The Hidden Window Mystery
#35: The Haunted Showboat
#36: The Secret of the Golden Pavilion
#37: The Clue in the Old Stagecoach
#38: The Mystery of the Fire Dragon
#39: The Clue of the Dancing Puppet
#40: The Moonstone Castle Mystery
#41: The Clue of the Whistling Bagpipes
#42: The Phantom of Pine Hill
#43: The Mystery of the 99 Steps
#44: The Clue in the Crossword Cipher
#45: The Spider Sapphire Mystery
#46: The Invisible Intruder
#47: The Mysterious Mannequin
#48: The Crooked Banister
#49: The Secret of Mirror Bay
#50: The Double Jinx Mystery
#51: Mystery of the Glowing Eye
#52: The Secret of the Forgotten City
#53: The Sky Phantom
#54: The Strange Message in the Parchment
#55: Mystery of Crocodile Island
#56: The Thirteenth Pearl
#57: The Triple Hoax
#58: The Flying Saucer Mystery
#59: The Secret in the Old Lace
#60: The Greek Symbol Mystery
#61: The Swami's Ring
#62: The Kachina Doll Mystery
#63: The Twin Dilemma
#64: Captive Witness

Nancy Drew Back-to-Back
#1: The Secret of the Old Clock/#2: The Hidden Staircase

Celebrate over 70 years with the World's Best Detective